The Bipolar Journey

Practical Strategies for Daily Life, Self-Care, Overcoming Stigma and Living BOLDLY

by

Ivette Smith

Contents

Copyright

Copyright © 2024 by Ivette Smith

All rights reserved.

No portion of this book may be reproduced in any form without written permission from the publisher or author, except as permitted by U.S. copyright law.

Paperback ISBN:978-1-970705-11-9

Introduction

The day I was diagnosed with bipolar disorder, I was sitting in a stark, off-white room with mahogany furniture that seemed far too bright, even though it was just like every other military hospital Senior Doctor's office. His words felt like they were dropped from a great height, smashing into my reality with the subtlety of a wrecking ball. I remember thinking, "Well, this is a new brand of Monday; my career is over." There was confusion, a creeping dread, but oddly, a sliver of relief too. Finally, there was a name for the chaos that had been my constant companion. I finally could explain the refinishing of furniture at 3 AM, or rearranging the living room furniture for no reason, skipping out on work, the shopping and spending sprees, the hypersexuality, the driving recklessly, and, of course, the depths of despair and agony at the thought that tomorrow would be another day if I were unlucky enough to wake up…

This book is born from these moments and countless others that followed. It's crafted to tell a story and be a companion on your journey. If you've just been handed a bipolar diagnosis or have been wrestling with it for years and are looking for fresh perspectives, this is for you. My aim? To light a path through the fog of fear and misinformation, to offer you hope and practical strategies, and to remind you fervently that this diagnosis does not define you. It's a part of your life, not the end of it.

I'm not a psychiatrist or psychologist. I don't wear a white coat, and my name doesn't follow with a string of impressive letters. But I have been where you are now. I've navigated the rocky terrains of this condition for over 30 years, and if there's one thing I've learned, it's that experience can be just as valuable as a medical degree. I'm here to share that experience with you—to offer insights from clinical studies and living a life full of ups and downs, victories and setbacks.

In these pages, we will explore the nooks and crannies of bipolar disorder—from deciphering the symptoms to managing medications and their side effects. We'll talk about the adjustments you might need to make to your lifestyle and how to handle the relationships that might feel more fragile now. And we'll do all of this with humor and light-heartedness because sometimes, laughter truly is the best medicine.

You're not alone on this path. This book is your invitation to a conversation, sharing stories and strategies that I hope will empower you. Together, we'll demystify the stigmas, tackle the hard questions, and find ways to explain your diagnosis without sending people running for the hills.

Let's not just survive with bipolar disorder; let's live with it, and let's live well. With actionable advice grounded in the latest research and my own life lessons, I promise to offer you tools that can make a real difference. Engage with this book, reflect on your experiences, and apply what resonates with your journey.

So, take a deep breath. You've got this, and I'm here to help. Let's redefine what it means to live with bipolar disorder, turning fear into knowledge and knowledge into power. Here's to finding light in unexpected places, and here's to you—more resilient and hopeful than you ever imagined possible.

Decoding Bipolar: Beyond the Diagnosis

Have you ever had one of those days where everything seems to flip upside-down? Well, getting diagnosed with bipolar disorder can feel a bit like that, but with a plot twist, you didn't see coming. You are the main character in a mystery novel, trying to decipher clues about your brain! Here we'll unravel some of those mysteries together, pulling back the curtain on the enigmatic world of bipolar disorder. From understanding the basics to getting a grip on the diagnosis process, consider this an insider's guide to navigating the stormy weather with a bit of humor and a lot of heart.

1.1 Bipolar Basics: Symptoms, Types, and Diagnosis

Understanding Symptoms

First things first, talk about symptoms. If bipolar disorder were a duo, its lead singers would be Mania and Depression, each rocking their unique style. Mania isn't just about feeling a bit energetic, it's like being on a caffeine buzz that won't quit. You might feel euphoric, full of grand plans, or irritably unstoppable. Then there's its counterpart, Depression. This isn't just a lousy day; it's like wading through molasses while wearing lead boots, with overwhelming sadness and fatigue and sometimes feeling hopelessly empty.

In the middle, playing a less intense set is Hypomania Mania's younger sibling. It's similar to mania but dialed down. You won't be scaling skyscrapers, but you might buzz with more energy than usual, which can feel either exhilarating or a bit out of control. Recognizing these symptoms in yourself or your loved ones can be like putting glasses on for the first time—suddenly, the blur becomes clear.

Classifying Bipolar Disorder

Now, onto the types—because not all bipolar disorders are created equal, we have Bipolar I, where mania takes the main stage for at least a week or is severe enough to need hospital care. There's

Bipolar II, where hypomania plays the opening act, followed by significant bouts of depression. Let's not forget about Cyclothymic Disorder, featuring at least two years of repeated mood changes, swinging from hypomanic symptoms to depressive symptoms without hitting full-blown highs or lows.

Getting these classifications right is crucial because every detail counts, just like any good thriller. Misclassifying can lead to the wrong management strategies, turning an already bumpy ride into an amusement park ride.

The Diagnosis Process

So, how do you pin down something as slippery as a bipolar diagnosis? Not through a simple blood test or a magic quiz. Diagnosis is more of an art form mixed with science. It typically starts with a comprehensive clinical interview by a mental health professional playing detective, gathering clues from your symptoms, medical history, and often input from family. Sometimes, they'll run tests to rule out other culprits like thyroid issues or to check medication levels. It's detective work, with you as the key witness.

Importance of Accurate Diagnosis

Why the fuss over getting the diagnosis spot-on? Well, think of it as getting the correct key for a lock. A precise diagnosis opens the door to effective management. It helps tailor the right treatment plan, whether medication, therapy, or lifestyle changes, ensuring that interventions are as effective as possible. An accurate diagnosis also helps set the stage for what to expect in your personal and professional life, paving the way for a clearer understanding of your experiences and needs.

Navigating the waters of bipolar disorder starts with understanding its fundamentals, cycles, and triggers. Knowledge makes you better equipped to advocate for yourself and make informed decisions. Remember, knowledge isn't just power it's empowerment. Let's put on those detective hats and continue to decode the mysteries of bipolar disorder together.

1.2 The Science Behind Bipolar: Neurobiology Made Simple

Imagine your brain is like a bustling city—neurons are the citizens, neurotransmitters are the messages they send each other, and the city's infrastructure is the brain's structure. In the world of bipolar disorder, this city experiences severe electrical storms (manic episodes) and power outages (depressive episodes) Let's simplify this complex neurobiology without needing a PhD to understand it.

Brain Chemistry and Bipolar

In the brain's dynamic hub, neurotransmitters like serotonin, dopamine, and norepinephrine are the primary messengers that communicate mood, energy levels, and emotional well-being. Think of dopamine as the brain's caffeine – it gets you up and running, fuels your highs, and, in excess, might make you feel like you're operating at warp speed during manic episodes. On the flip side, when there's a drop in this and other neurotransmitters like serotonin, it's akin to the coffee running out before your day does, potentially ushering in a period of depression.

In bipolar disorder, the regulation of these neurotransmitters gets skewed. The result? A neurological seesaw that swings between the extremes of emotional highs and lows. This imbalance isn't just about feeling good or bad, but a profound disturbance in the brain's natural rhythm, which affects overall functioning.

Research Insights

Recent studies have thrown a spotlight on the complexity of bipolar disorder, debunking myths that it's just a mood swing thing that can be snapped out of. Advanced imaging studies show that some regions of the brain might be structurally and functionally different in those with bipolar disorder compared to those without. For instance, areas like the prefrontal cortex – the brain's command center for decision-making, judgment, and problem-solving – often show variations in activity. This insight helps explain why someone with bipolar disorder might make impulsive decisions during a manic episode or struggle to make any decisions during a depressive phase.

Moreover, research utilizing functional MRI (fMRI) has observed how the brain behaves during tasks involving emotional processing, revealing distinctive patterns in people with bipolar disorder. These groundbreaking insights are crucial as they guide the development of more targeted treatments beyond symptom management to address the root neurological issues.

Genes vs. Environment

The age-old debate of nature versus nurture also plays a significant role in bipolar disorder. Genetically, if bipolar disorder were a novel, it would be a saga filled with complex characters; multiple genes contribute to the risk, each adding their twist to the plot. No single gene "causes" bipolar disorder, but the interaction of many genes can significantly increase the likelihood of developing the condition.

Environmentally, think of your life experiences as the weather affecting that bustling city in your brain. Certain life events or stressors, like relationship troubles, loss of a loved one, or extreme stress, might not cause bipolar disorder directly but can trigger its onset in someone already genetically predisposed. These experiences flip a switch, and the city's usual operations spiral into electrical storms or power outages.

Future Directions

Looking ahead, the horizon is promising in bipolar disorder research. Scientists are delving into not only the genetic and environmental causes but also revolutionary treatments that could more precisely recalibrate the brain's faulty wiring. One exciting frontier is personalized medicine, driven by genetic testing, which tailors treatments to individual patients, potentially enhancing treatment efficacy and reducing side effects.

Furthermore, ongoing research into brain plasticity offers hope that even with a genetic predisposition, the brain can learn new patterns of activity that promote stability rather than extremes of mood. Potential biomarkers are also being explored, which could lead to earlier detection and intervention, shifting the narrative from crisis management to prevention and maintenance.

Understanding the neurobiology of bipolar disorder sets the stage for more effective interventions and significantly shifts the narrative from blame and misunderstanding to one of empathy and precision in care. As we continue to unravel the intricate tapestry of brain function, genetics, and environmental impacts, the future looks increasingly hopeful for those affected by bipolar disorder, providing clarity and new tools to manage and thrive despite the challenges.

1.3 Debunking Myths: What Bipolar Disorder Isn't

Let's set the record straight on a few things. If confusion were a sport, the myths surrounding bipolar disorder would have a pretty good shot at taking home the gold. From wild misconceptions to oversimplified stereotypes, it's high time we tackled this head-on because understanding what bipolar disorder isn't is just as crucial as understanding what it is.

Myth vs. Reality

First up, the classic mix-up: "Bipolar means split personality." Nope, not even close. Bipolar disorder is about experiencing significant mood swings that include emotional highs (mania or hypomania) and lows (depression), not having two distinct personalities. This common misunderstanding might stem from the word "bipolar," suggesting a split between two poles or extremes, let's be clear—this is about variations in mood, not identity.

Then there's the big one: "People with bipolar can't lead normal lives." Now, this is not only false but also incredibly dismissive. Sure, managing bipolar disorder presents its unique set of challenges, but with. Still, with the proper treatment and strategies, many people with bipolar disorder hold down fulfilling jobs, maintain healthy relationships, and lead rich, productive lives. It's not about living a 'normal' life, it's about living your life and living it well, regardless of a diagnosis.

Stigma and Misunderstandings

Speaking of misconceptions, the stigma around bipolar disorder can feel like a pesky shadow you can't shake. This stigma stems mainly from a lack of understanding and loads of misinformation. People hear "bipolar" and think of unpredictability, instability, or worse, unreliability. This stigma can lead to people with bipolar disorder feeling isolated, misunderstood, and even discriminated against, which can prevent them from seeking the help they need.

Challenging, educating, and shining a light on these shadows is crucial. By speaking openly about what bipolar disorder is, sharing stories, and spreading accurate information, we can chip away at the misconceptions and make it easier for people to seek support without fear of judgment.

Bipolar Disorder and Violence

Now let's tackle a particularly damaging myth: the idea that bipolar disorder inherently leads to violent behavior. Studies consistently show that most people with mental health conditions, including bipolar disorder, are no more violent than the general population. They are more likely to be victims of violence than perpetrators. It's essential to look at these statistics head-on to dismantle the baseless fears that can surround mental health diagnoses. This isn't just about correcting false information; it's about changing how society perceives and treats those with bipolar disorder.

The Role of Media

Lastly, let's talk about the elephant in the room—the media. Films, TV shows, and even news reports can sometimes paint those with bipolar disorder as caricatures—unpredictable, over-the-top, or tragic figures. While there's been some progress in recent years, with more nuanced portrayals and greater sensitivity, there's still a long way to go. The media influences perceptions and can be a formidable ally in educating the public and combating stigma.

Take, for instance, a popular TV show that portrays a character with bipolar disorder. If the character is well-rounded, their condition accurately represented, and their challenges met with empathy and support from others, it can foster understanding and compassion in the audience. On the flip side, sensationalized or inaccurate portrayals can reinforce stereotypes and widen the gap of misunderstanding.

When we encounter these portrayals in our everyday lives, it's valuable to engage critically, questioning and discussing their accuracy and impact. Whether writing a thoughtful blog post, sharing insights on social media, or simply discussing it with friends and family, every conversation can be a step towards greater understanding.

As we continue to pull apart the myths and shine a light on the realities, remember it's about fostering empathy, challenging stereotypes, and creating a more informed and understanding society. Whether you're living with bipolar disorder or know someone who is, the power of knowledge and the strength of a community can make all the difference. Let's keep the conversation going, debunk myths, and build bridges of understanding, one truth at a time.

1.4 Bipolar I vs. Bipolar II: Navigating the Differences

Ah, the tale of two bipolars. When you first hear about Bipolar I and II, it might sound like a sequel in a film franchise—when you thought you understood the plot, along comes a twist! However, understanding these types is crucial in managing the condition effectively. Let's break it down: Bipolar I is the blockbuster of the series, known for its full-blown manic episodes. These aren't just spurts of high energy or enthusiasm; we're talking about intense, week-long (at least) escapades where sleep becomes a forgotten concept, decisions are made at the speed of light, and grand, often unrealistic plans are set into motion. To meet the criteria for Bipolar I, a person must have experienced at least one of these manic episodes, which episodes of depression might follow. However, the latter isn't a requirement for diagnosis.

Conversely, Bipolar II might be seen as the less intense sequel, but trust me, it's no less impactful. It features hypomania, a milder form of mania that's not as extreme or potentially disruptive as full mania. People experiencing hypomania can often still go about their daily routines. However, the catch with Bipolar II is the significant periods of depression that tag along. These episodes are frequently more profound, longer, and more disabling than those experienced in Bipolar I.

There is a third category, sometimes referred to as Bipolar III. It is Cyclothymia, and the episodes are not as extreme as those in Bipolar I or II. Now, why does this matter? Picture this: you're trying to solve a problem, if you have the wrong formula the results will not be accurate. It helps immensely to know what you're dealing with. Treating Bipolar I with strategies better suited for Bipolar II (or vice versa) can be like using a screwdriver on a nail—technically possible, but unnecessarily frustrating and ineffective. For Bipolar I, treatment often prioritizes controlling the highs of mania and might include a combination of mood stabilizers and antipsychotic medications. The approach is somewhat aggressive because unchecked mania can lead to risky behaviors and significant life disruptions.

Treatment for Bipolar II, meanwhile, tends to focus heavily on managing depression while keeping an eye on the milder hypomanic episodes. This might involve a different balance of medications, like using antidepressants with mood stabilizers to prevent a swing into hypomania. It's a delicate dance, requiring precise tunes and steps to maintain the right rhythm.

Living with each type of Bipolar disorder also dishes out its unique set of daily challenges and strategies. With Bipolar I, the unpredictability of manic episodes can feel like walking a tightrope without knowing when the wind might gust. Strategies here often involve strict adherence to medication schedules, regular therapy sessions, and developing a strong awareness of one's mood shifts to mitigate the mania before it takes the stage; it's about prevention, preparation, and quick action.

For those managing Bipolar II, the long shadows of depression make it crucial to have robust support systems and coping mechanisms in play, so it's less about bracing for the occasional storm and more about continually nurturing one's mental garden to keep the weeds of depression from taking root. This might mean regular exercise, maintaining a consistent sleep schedule, and perhaps most importantly, staying connected with supportive friends, family, or support groups who can provide light during darker times.

Navigating Bipolar I and II requires not just knowledge but also patience and personalization in treatment and lifestyle adjustments. Each type has its traits, challenges, and nuances, making it essential to tailor your approach—be it through medication, therapy, or daily habits—to suit the specific type you or your loved one is dealing with. Understanding these differences enables better management, smoother sailing, and a more stable life despite the ups and downs. So, while the differences between Bipolar I and II can be subtle, they are incredibly significant in crafting a life that acknowledges the highs and lows but isn't defined by them. And with the proper knowledge and tools at your disposal, navigating these waters becomes a part of the adventure, not the whole story.

1.5 The Role of Genetics and Environment in Bipolar Disorder

Let's talk about what's brewing in your genetic cocktail and how your environment plays a role in the mix. It's like understanding the recipe that makes up your unique flavor of bipolar disorder. You might think that genes are the all-powerful directors behind the scenes, while your environment is just the stage setting. But in reality, it's way more interactive—think of it as a dynamic play where genes and environment constantly improvise.

Genetic Factors

Diving into the pool of genetics, it's clear that bipolar disorder doesn't play favorites; it tends to run in families, suggesting a solid genetic thread. Research pinpoints that if you have a relative with Bipolar disorder, your likelihood of developing the condition is higher. However, it's not a straightforward inheritance like passing down a family heirloom. It's more like a lottery—having the genes increases your chances but doesn't guarantee the jackpot of developing the disorder.

Scientists have been mapping the human genome and found several genes that are more common in populations with Bipolar disorder. These genes often play crucial roles in the brain's communication systems. Also, it's not just one single gene at fault here; it's more likely a team effort with multiple genes, each adding its own little twist to how bipolar disorder manifests in an individual. This complexity is why predicting or preventing the disorder using genetic information alone isn't currently feasible. However, understanding these genetic influences helps us grasp why bipolar disorder can appear in different shades and intensities in other people.

Environmental Triggers

Now let's set the stage with environmental factors. These are the life experiences and external conditions that can trigger the onset of Bipolar disorder symptoms or influence the course of the disorder. Common triggers include stressful life events like the loss of a loved one, a breakup, or significant career changes. Even seemingly positive stressors, like getting married or starting a new job, can spark symptoms if they shake up your world significantly.

Imagine your genetic predisposition as a loaded spring. Environmental stressors are like weights added to that spring. Add enough weight, and the spring might snap, triggering the onset of bipolar disorder symptoms. This analogy helps explain why two people with similar genetic risks might have different experiences; it all depends on the weights added to their respective springs.

Nature vs. Nurture Debate

The age-old debate of nature versus nurture is particularly poignant in bipolar disorder. It's not about whether genetics or environment are more important; it's about how they interact. Think of it as a dance between your internal genetic makeup and external life experiences. Sometimes, genetics take the lead; other times, environmental factors dictate the next move. This dance can determine the onset, severity, and very nature of the disorder in an individual.

For instance, someone might carry the genetic predisposition for bipolar disorder but remain symptom-free until they encounter severe psychological stress or substance abuse, which then triggers the condition. On the other hand, someone with less genetic risk might experience the same stressors but never develop bipolar disorder. This interplay suggests that while you can't change your genetics, managing your environment and how you respond to stress can significantly influence disorder's impact on your life.

Family History and Risk

If Bipolar disorder is a typical guest in your family tree, you might wonder about your own risk or that of your children. First, breathe—having a family history increases risk, it's not destiny. It's more about awareness and management. If you know there's a history of bipolar disorder in your family, you can be vigilant about the signs and symptoms. Early intervention is critical in managing bipolar disorder effectively, and being aware of the risk can help you and your healthcare provider make informed decisions about your mental health.

For those with a family history, consider regular mental health check-ups. Think of them like tune-ups for your mind. They provide a space to discuss any potential symptoms or concerns early on, similar to how you might manage a risk for diabetes or heart disease. Educating yourself and your family about the disorder also demystifies it and can prepare everyone to handle it better if it does show up.

Understanding the roles of genetics and environment in bipolar disorder does not just illuminate the pathways of risk and management; it empowers you to navigate these complex terrains with knowledge and proactive strategies. Whether tweaking lifestyle factors to manage stress better or engaging in therapy to unpack and mitigate potential triggers, you have the tools to influence how this interplay affects your life. So, keep this information close as you tailor your approach to living with or preventing Bipolar disorder, making informed choices that enhance your well-being and resilience in the face of genetic and environmental challenges.

1.6 Understanding Mood Episodes: From Mania to Depression

Mania, in the realm of Bipolar disorder isn't just about having a surplus of energy it's like riding a roller-coaster that only goes up. The signs of a manic episode can range from euphoria, excessive talking, and bursts of creative ideas to irritability, reckless decisions, and a diminished need for sleep. Imagine feeling so invincible that you decide to start five new business ventures in a week or impulsively book a flight to a country you can't even pronounce—these aren't just quirky anecdotes; they are real-life manifestations of mania that can have serious, lasting consequences. This heightened state of activity and mood can lead to decisions that make sense at the moment but are disastrous in hindsight. The impact on behavior and decision-making is profound, affecting not only the individual but also their relationships and professional life. The fallout from these decisions can linger long after the manic episode subsides, often leaving a trail of personal and financial chaos.

Then, as if the body and mind tire from all that upward momentum, the inevitable crash into depression occurs. It isn't just sadness; this is a profound, pervasive low that can feel like all color has drained from the world. Bipolar depression differs from unipolar depression (the kind often experienced in major depressive disorder) in its relationship with manic episodes. In bipolar disorder, the depths of depression are usually more profound and more complex because they follow these extreme highs. The effects are debilitating: overwhelming feelings of hopelessness, a loss of interest in almost everything, and sometimes, thoughts of self-harm or suicide. It's a stark contrast to the occasionally exhilarating, frenzied highs of mania, and it can leave individuals feeling like they are living two different lives.

Mixed episodes, or mixed states, add another layer of complexity. Here, symptoms of mania and depression mix in a confusing cocktail. Imagine feeling energetically sad or despairingly impulsive—these paradoxical feelings can coexist in a mixed episode. This blending of highs and lows can make diagnosis and treatment particularly challenging. The mixed state is a turbulent weather system of emotion, where sun and storm clouds collide, leaving the individual unsure of which way the wind is blowing. These episodes are particularly risky, as the combination of depressive hopelessness and manic energy can increase the risk of suicide.

The cyclical nature of bipolar disorder, with its rotation of high, low, and sometimes mixed episodes, underscores the critical need for long-term management strategies. Recognizing the patterns in these cycles can be like learning to predict the weather—a skill that, while never perfect, can significantly mitigate the disorder's impact. Long-term management might include medication to stabilize mood, therapy to develop coping strategies, and lifestyle adjustments to promote stability. It also involves building a strong support network that can help during all weather conditions—the manic highs, the depressive lows, or the confusing mixed states.

Understanding these episodes in their entirety—recognizing their signs, symptoms, and the challenges they bring—is crucial. It's not just about weathering the storm; it's about preparing for it, knowing when it might arrive, and having the tools ready to ensure it causes as little disruption as possible. Recognizing early signs can often mean the difference between a minor disturbance and a major upheaval. In the world of Bipolar disorder, knowledge and preparation are key. With the right strategies and supports in place, the roller-coaster can be less daunting and the weather less fearsome, allowing for a life that embraces all its seasons.

The Common Symptoms of Bipolar Depression

- Feelings of worthlessness or guilt
- Weight loss or gain (due to changes in how much you eat)
- Depressed mood most of the day
- Loss of interest in things you once enjoyed
- Trouble falling or staying asleep or sleeping too much
- Feeling irritated easily
- Fatigue or loss of energy
- Difficulty thinking, concentrating, and making decisions
- Thoughts of harming yourself

The Initial Aftermath: Coping with Diagnosis

Imagine you've just been handed a jigsaw puzzle, except the pieces aren't neatly boxed, and the picture you're supposed to assemble isn't on the lid—it's locked away in a vault. That's a bit of what it feels like to receive a bipolar diagnosis. Suddenly, you have all these pieces: symptoms, treatments, and advice, but none seem to fit together easily. Well, consider this chapter your guide to starting that puzzle, one piece at a time, with a dash of humor and a whole lot of understanding.

2.1 Just Diagnosed: Now What?

Initial Reactions

So, the doctor just dropped the B-word—Bipolar. You might feel like you've just been cast in a thriller, not necessarily one you auditioned for. It's OK. It's normal. It's expected. From the moment those words hit the air, you might feel a storm of emotions swirling inside—relief because finally, there's a name for the ride you've been on; fear because what does this label mean for your future; confusion because what even is bipolar disorder, really; or even denial, because surely, this must be a mistake.

These feelings? They don't just validate your experience; they are a universal ticket every person diagnosed with bipolar disorder holds. You're not alone in this cinema of chaos. Acknowledging these emotions is the first step towards managing them. It's like the opening scene of your personal epic—intense, yes, but essential for setting the stage for what comes next.

First Steps to Take

Now, onto the action plan. Think of it as your own movie montage—cutting between scenes of you gearing up to take control. First off, education is your armor. Understanding Bipolar disorder robs it of some of its terror. Dive into reputable sources—books, medical journals, or trusted websites like the National Institute of Mental

Health or the International Bipolar Foundation. Knowledge is power, and in your case, it's also strategy.

Next, assemble your crew. More than likely, your primary care provider or family doctor diagnosed you and will now refer you to a specialist for evaluation and treatment. A psychiatrist isn't just a doctor; they're more like a guide through this new terrain you're navigating. They can help customize your treatment plan, including medication, therapy, or both. A psychologist may be better suited for therapy, but you need a psychiatrist to prescribe medication. This step is about crafting your sword tailored to your battle. Sometimes, we carry around a little more emotional and mental baggage. This baggage can be more detrimental to someone with Bipolar because not only do you have to manage the illness but also deal with the lurking skeletons in the proverbial closet.

The Importance of Support

As you gear up for this journey, remember that every hero needs a fellowship—think Frodo and his gang. It's time to rally your support system. This crew can be family, friends, or even others who've been diagnosed with bipolar disorder. There's also immense strength in connecting with bipolar support groups, where you can share your experiences and learn from others who are walking similar paths These people aren't just your supporters, allies, confidantes, and cheerleaders. They're the ones who will see you through the plot twists and cliffhangers.

Self-Care Practices

Finally, let's talk about your daily training regimen—self-care. These aren't just spa days and smoothies (though those are nice!) It's about constructing a routine that includes regular sleep, balanced nutrition, physical activity, and, yes, mental breaks. Start simple. Maybe it's setting a bedtime, finding time for a walk, or carving out moments for meditation or journaling. Consider these the daily drills that keep you in shape for the main event—managing bipolar disorder. Establishing a routine will better help you track mood changes or potential triggers. If you are like me, you will resist therapy, exercising, and good eating habits—heck, I didn't do it before Bipolar; what makes anyone think I'll part with Haagen Dazs now?!

My path started in the basement of rock bottom. In a mild depression, around the end of 2020, the depression got progressively worse for the following year. Yes, a year. But I can't put it all at the feet of my diagnosis. I was injured at work and had to resign from an enjoyable job. Other plans fell apart one by one, including all attempts at finding a new job. Savings were dwindling, bills were mounting, and all my poor husband could do was watch me implode. Then, of course, the little things in life would not be left behind, so the toilet would back up, the car would drop the transmission, and the cat would decide to do its business in the middle of the kitchen. I mean, really?!

I finally started walking 10-15 minutes daily on the treadmill, sometimes with tears in my eyes, and noticed it made me feel better, so I kept it up for a while. Slowly, I worked for up to 45 minutes and then got bored. I couldn't forget the good feelings I got out of exercising, so I went to the internet to see what I could find. I had played with Pinterest for Christmas decorations a while back, so I started exploring the site further. I found many interesting things, and handmade journals caught my eye. Mind you, I didn't (still don't) believe I had an artistic gene in me. I could not draw a straight line with a ruler. You can find almost anything on Pinterest. I started noticing quotes and funny memes, and it felt less toxic than other platforms, so I started writing in the journals, and wow! I had so much to say, even if, especially, because no one would ever read these.

Reflective Pause

Take a moment here. Reflect on these initial steps. They're your foundation, your starting blocks. Each one is a move towards understanding, managing, and thriving with bipolar disorder. Write down one action you can take today from each of these steps. It could be as simple as bookmarking a medical site, calling a friend, or deciding tonight's bedtime. Small steps, significant strides.

2.2 Managing the Emotional Roller-coaster Post-Diagnosis

So, you've received your diagnosis, and suddenly, you're on this emotional see-saw, right? One minute you're up, the next you're down, and sometimes you're just hanging upside down, wondering which way is up. Managing these swings is like being the conductor of your emotional symphony—sometimes the music is harmonious, and other times, it's just cacophony. Let's talk about how to turn that chaos into a melody, starting with some solid emotional regulation techniques.

Mindfulness and cognitive behavioral strategies are your instruments here. I was hoping you wouldn't roll your eyes; although I have tried some of these, they are not mantras, incense, oils, or crystals. Think of mindfulness as your metronome, helping you keep pace with your thoughts and feelings without getting swept away. It's about sitting with your emotions and observing them like clouds passing in the sky—noticeable but not necessarily impactful. You can practice this through simple daily meditations or even mindful walking. Focus on being present, feeling each step and breath, and letting those intrusive thoughts stroll by. Look around and breathe with intent. Cognitive Behavioral Therapy (CBT), on the other hand, is like tuning your instrument. It helps you challenge and change those distorted thoughts and behaviors that throw you off-key. For instance, if you find yourself thinking, "This diagnosis means my life is over," CBT techniques teach you to reframe those thoughts to something more balanced and accurate, like, "This diagnosis is a challenge, but I can manage it with the right strategies."

Now, let's talk about navigating the fog of uncertainty that comes post-diagnosis. It's perfectly normal to feel like you're treading water in the ocean of "What ifs?" What if I can't manage this? What if it changes how people see me? Here's where building a mindset geared towards resilience and hope comes into play. Start by setting small, achievable goals each day. This could be anything from reading one chapter of a book on bipolar disorder to going for a 10-minute walk. Each small victory is a lighthouse guiding you through the mist, showing you that you can manage this, one step at a time. Also, keep a gratitude journal. I can tell you my journals were NOT about being grateful. They were dark, bitter, and full of barbs, giving the universe the finger most of the time. There were everyday challenges to write down three things I was grateful for. On more harrowing days, these notes were powerful reminders of the good still around me and how I climbed the previous rungs in the ladder.

Therapy can often be daunting, but think of it as finding a co-navigator for your journey through uncharted waters. A therapist specializing in bipolar disorder isn't just a clinician; they're a confidant, a strategist, and sometimes, a lifeline. In therapy, you have a safe space to unpack all the baggage you've been carrying. You can explore your feelings about the diagnosis, dissect your fears, and construct coping strategies in a structured environment. It's not about getting advice but about gaining clarity and tools to help you adjust your sails as you navigate these new seas.

Finally, let's consider the process of building a new normal. This isn't about returning to who you were before the diagnosis; it's about creating a life that acknowledges and accommodates your new reality. Start by integrating your treatment plan into your daily routine. Make your medication schedule as routine as your morning coffee. Build check-ins that match your mood as regularly as your nightly TV show binge. Then, slowly weave your personal goals and interests back into your life. Love painting? Set up a small studio corner in your home where you can dive into colors when you feel up to it. Passionate about writing? Start a blog about your journey with bipolar disorder. This new normal might look different but can still be uniquely and wonderfully yours. It's about creating a harmonious symphony, where bipolar disorder has a note, but it's not the entire melody.

2.3 Telling Your Loved Ones: Strategies and Tips

So, you've got this new piece of information about yourself—bipolar disorder. It's like suddenly finding out you're part secret agent, part mystery novel protagonist. Now comes one of the trickier parts of the plot: sharing this news with your loved ones. Deciding when and whom to tell about your diagnosis can feel like choosing the right moment to drop a plot twist in a story. It's essential, and timing is everything. You might want to consider telling those closest to you first or those who you think will provide the support you need. It's like casting characters for a pivotal scene. You wouldn't want someone who'll overreact or underreact in a crucial moment. Consider their personalities, the quality of your relationship, and their capacity to offer support.

When you're ready to share, picking a calm, private setting to talk without interruptions is vital. This isn't a conversation to have in the middle of a family barbecue or via text message. You want space where emotions can be expressed, and questions can be asked freely. Be prepared for a range of reactions. Some might take it in stride; others might be confused or upset. Remember, their first reactions aren't their final word—they're the beginning of a conversation. Just as you had time to adjust to your diagnosis, they'll need time, too.

Explaining Bipolar disorder in clear, simple terms can help demystify your condition. Avoid medical jargon. Instead, try comparing it to something more relatable. You could say, "Imagine your brain is like a car, and most people's brains have reliable brakes and steady acceleration. My brain's features are a bit more unpredictable, which can make my moods and energy levels very high or very low. Treatment is like regular maintenance that helps keep the car—and me—running smoothly." Emphasize that bipolar disorder is manageable with treatment and that you're learning more about how to handle it every day. This helps frame your condition in a context that's not just about challenges but also solutions and management. Your loved ones may already have known "something was up," and it's a matter of including them in your new goals.

As you navigate through their reactions, prepare yourself for a mix of support and misunderstanding. Some might offer help immediately; others might pull away, unsure what to say or do. Some might even deny that you have a disorder at all. It's natural for people to react based on their perceptions of mental health, which are shaped by personal beliefs, stigma, and misinformation. If you encounter a reaction rooted in stigma or myth, use it as an opportunity to educate. You could say, "I know some people think that bipolar disorder means I'm unstable, but it's more like having a condition that I can manage with medication and therapy, much like diabetes."

In the end, embracing the support from your loved ones while setting necessary boundaries is crucial. Let them know precisely how they can help you. Maybe you need them to be more patient during your low phases, or perhaps you need them to listen without trying to fix things. At the same time, it's OK to set boundaries around your mental health. If specific topics or comments make you uncomfortable, it's OK to say, "I appreciate your concern, but I'm not comfortable discussing that right now." This helps establish a supportive dialogue that respects your needs and boundaries.

Telling your loved ones about your bipolar diagnosis isn't just about sharing a part of your life; it's about inviting them to support you in a meaningful, informed way. It strengthens connections, dispels myths, and builds a network of support that will be invaluable as you manage your bipolar disorder. It's about letting them walk with you, equipped with understanding and compassion, as you navigate this part of your life. Remember, you're not handing them a burden; you're offering them a chance to be there for you, just as you would be for them.

2.4 Building Your Bipolar Management Toolkit

Imagine you're setting up a workshop. This isn't just any workshop—it's one where you craft your well-being, and each tool you add is customized to help manage your bipolar disorder effectively. Think of this as assembling your mental health toolkit, a collection of practical resources designed to keep the machine running smoothly, even during those unpredictable moments.

Essential Tools and Resources

First, let's talk about gadgets and gizmos—a.k.a. tools and apps—that can make managing bipolar disorder a bit like having a high-tech assistant on your side. A mood tracker is your go-to tool. Apps like Daylio or eMoods allow you to log your daily mood swings, sleep patterns, and medication adherence. These apps are like having a personal mood diary in your pocket, providing insights and patterns you might miss in the daily hustle. Over time, you'll see trends to help you and your healthcare provider make informed decisions about your treatment plan.

Then there are educational websites, which serve as your encyclopedia. Websites like Psych Central or the Depression and Bipolar Support Alliance offer a wealth of articles, webinars, and forums where you can learn more about Bipolar disorder and connect with others who share similar experiences. These resources are like chapters in a guidebook, offering new strategies, scientific updates, and personal stories that can illuminate different aspects of living with bipolar disorder.

Creating a Treatment Plan

Now, let's sketch out your blueprint—a personalized treatment plan. This isn't something you whip up in an afternoon. It's a detailed, thought-out plan created with your healthcare provider. Think of it as a recipe where the ingredients include your medication, therapy sessions, lifestyle adjustments, and any other interventions that suit your needs. The key here is customization. What works for one person might not work for another, so your treatment plan must reflect your unique situation, symptoms, and goals.

This plan should also be flexible. Just as a pilot adjusts a flight path due to weather changes, be prepared to tweak your treatment plan as you go along. This might mean adjusting dosages, trying new therapies, or shifting focus from one area to another based on how you respond to different treatments. Regular check-ins with your doctor are like those strategic meetings where you review what's working and what's not, ensuring that every element of the plan contributes effectively to your stability.

Emergency Planning

No matter how well you maintain your car, sometimes, you might still find yourself with a flat tire. That's why you need an emergency kit. In the context of bipolar management, this includes having a crisis plan in place. This plan should include contact information for your healthcare provider, a trusted friend or family member, and a local or national crisis hotline like the National Suicide Prevention Lifeline. Keep this information easily accessible—maybe in your wallet, on your fridge, or saved prominently on your phone. Just knowing it's there can provide a sense of security.

Additionally, inform a few trusted individuals about your emergency plan. These people can step in if you cannot manage on your own. They should know how to recognize the signs you're struggling with and clearly understand how they can best support you—whether helping you contact your doctor, staying with you until help arrives, or just being there to listen.

Lifestyle Adjustments for Stability

Lastly, let's fine-tune the machine by making lifestyle adjustments that promote stability. Sleep hygiene is your foundation. Try to stick to a regular sleep schedule, as sleep disruptions can trigger mood episodes. Create a bedtime routine that signals to your body it's time to wind down, perhaps by reading or meditating before bed.

Your diet also plays a role in your mental health. Foods rich in omega-3 fatty acids, like salmon and flaxseeds, can be beneficial, while a balanced diet helps stabilize your energy levels throughout the day. Regular physical activity is equally important. Exercise isn't just good for your body; it's a natural mood stabilizer. Even something as simple as a daily walk can significantly affect how you feel.

Incorporating these tools into your daily life creates a structured environment that supports your mental health. This doesn't mean rigidity; it's about creating a flexible framework that adjusts as your needs change. By building and continually updating your bipolar management toolkit, you're equipped not just to cope with Bipolar disorder but to thrive despite it.

2.5 Seeking Professional Help: Finding the Right Team for You

When it comes to managing Bipolar disorder, think of yourself as the director of a blockbuster movie. You've got a vision (your health goals) and a script (your treatment plan), but you need a stellar cast and crew to bring it all to life. This is where finding the right healthcare providers comes into play. Imagine you're casting for the critical roles in your support system movie. You wouldn't just pick any actor off the street, right? You want the Meryl Streep and Tom Hanks of healthcare—professionals who know their lines and can deliver them with empathy and expertise.

First up, your lead actors are the psychiatrist and psychologist. A psychiatrist is like the director of photography, helping to set the mood right with the appropriate treatment modalities, medication, or other medical interventions. When choosing a psychiatrist, look for someone with a track record in treating bipolar disorder. Their experience in navigating the complex landscape of mood disorders can make a significant difference in your treatment effectiveness. On the other hand, a psychologist, like a scriptwriter, delves deep into your experiences, helping you rewrite narratives that might not be serving you well anymore. They specialize in therapy to help you understand and manage how you think, behave, and react.

But this isn't just a two-person show. The multidisciplinary approach includes a variety of healthcare professionals who each bring their unique skills to the stage. Depending on your plan and financial means, you might consider a nutritionist as your production designer, setting the scene with a mood-stabilizing diet, or a personal trainer like a stunt coordinator helping you build strength and resilience. Each professional plays a pivotal role, and together, they ensure that every aspect of your health is addressed, making the management of bipolar disorder more comprehensive and integrated.

As you assemble this award-winning cast, you must audition them thoroughly. Here are some key questions to ask: What's your experience with bipolar disorder? How do you approach treatment? Can you outline how you'd customize my care? What's your policy on communication between sessions? These questions can help gauge whether their approach aligns with your needs and expectations, ensuring the professional relationship is comfortable and beneficial.

Navigating insurance and costs in healthcare can often feel like trying to understand tax law when all you did was a weekend course on personal finance. It's complex and, sometimes, downright frustrating. Start by understanding your insurance coverage. What does it cover? Are your preferred providers and treatments covered? If the jargon gets too much, customer service is your go-to. Remember, no question is too small regarding your health and finances.

For those navigating these waters without insurance, consider looking into sliding scale fee structures offered by many therapists, which adjust the cost based on your income. Community clinics and training institutions often provide services at a lower cost as part of their training programs. Additionally, online platforms can offer more affordable therapy options; some even provide subscriptions that make frequent sessions more economically feasible.

Building your healthcare team is about creating a circle of trust and expertise around you. Each member, from psychiatrist to therapist, from nutritionist to yoga instructor, plays a critical role in your well-being. Like in any good movie, every role is crucial, and how well the cast performs together can turn a good story into a great one. So take your time, choose wisely, and build a team that turns your health journey into a masterpiece.

2.6 Setting Realistic Goals and Expectations

After receiving a bipolar diagnosis, it can feel like you're suddenly supposed to become the CEO of a company called My Bipolar Life Inc. overnight. And like any good CEO, you need a strategic plan, right? Well, that's where setting realistic, achievable goals comes into play. It's not about plotting out your entire life trajectory in one evening but instead establishing manageable, bite-sized goals that steer you toward wellness and stability. Think of it as setting waypoints on a map to your preferred destination, knowing that you might sometimes take a scenic route or hit an unexpected detour.

Setting goals post-diagnosis is crucial because it gives you something concrete to work towards amidst the often overwhelming sea of information and emotions. These goals can be as simple as taking your medication at the same time every day, attending all scheduled therapy sessions for the month, or even just dedicating fifteen minutes a day to a relaxing activity like reading or meditation. The key here is flexibility—life with bipolar disorder is often unpredictable, and your goals need to be adaptable enough to accommodate the ebbs and flows of your condition. This flexibility helps reduce frustration and discouragement since you're not rigidly bound to a set of expectations that might not always align with the realities of living with bipolar disorder.

Now, let's talk about adjusting those expectations. It's easy to fall into the trap of idealizing treatment outcomes or expecting linear progress without setbacks. However, the nature of bipolar disorder means that the path to stability often includes some degree of trial and error, whether in finding the proper medication, the most effective therapeutic approaches, or the ideal lifestyle adjustments. Emphasizing progress over perfection allows you to celebrate the small victories along the way—a crucial component in building momentum and maintaining motivation. For instance, if you've managed to keep your appointments and stick to your medication schedule, that's a win, even if you still have bad days.

Celebrating milestones, no matter how small, reinforces a positive feedback loop. Did you endure a tough week without canceling a single therapy session? That's a milestone. Have you communicated your feelings during a mood swing more effectively than before? Another milestone. These celebrations can be simple acknowledgments or small rewards, like treating yourself to a movie night. They remind you of your progress and resilience, which are essential for fostering hope and motivation. They are the proof that despite the ups and downs, you are moving forward, one foot in front of the other.

Looking at the long-term outlook, it's logical to acknowledge that while bipolar disorder is a lifelong condition, it is also one that can be managed effectively with the proper treatment and strategies. Many people with bipolar disorder lead rich, fulfilling lives marked by successful careers, rewarding relationships, and vibrant social lives. The key lies in ongoing management, which includes consistent medication adherence, regular therapy, and a stable support system. This doesn't mean there won't be challenging days or even relapses. However, with each challenge comes an opportunity to learn more about managing the condition, refining your strategies, and continuing to evolve your approach to living with bipolar disorder.

Remember to be kind to yourself when setting goals and expectations for your life post-diagnosis. You are learning to navigate a new aspect of your life that requires patience, perseverance, and self-compassion. Each step forward, no matter how small, is a piece of the puzzle fitting into place, gradually revealing a picture of a life not defined by bipolar disorder but enhanced by the depth, resilience, and understanding it brings.

As this chapter closes, we've equipped ourselves with realistic goals, adjusted our expectations, and prepared to celebrate every small victory on the path to managing bipolar disorder. These strategies are not just about coping; they're about thriving. They remind us that each step forward enriches our journey, offering valuable lessons and deeper insights into both the challenges and triumphs of living with bipolar disorder. With these tools in hand, we turn the page, ready to explore deeper into the practicalities and personal adjustments that make navigating this path not only possible but also profoundly rewarding.

Psychiatric Meds 101

This chapter aims to dispel common misconceptions surrounding psychiatric medications. While some individuals harbor reservations about medication use, others, like myself, rely on them for daily functioning. Dismissing the effectiveness of drugs as not being 'real' is unfounded. Medications offer respite to the brain from operating under abnormal conditions. There is skepticism toward pharmaceutical companies due to misleading marketing or a lack of transparency regarding a product's efficacy. Additionally, there is debate over symptom management versus disease eradication and whether specific side effects that do not go away are worth the discomfort.

3.1 Understanding Psychiatric Medications

Understanding how these medications work is like unraveling the mystery behind a magic trick. It's about making the complex simple. For instance, mood stabilizers ensure optimal communication between nerves in the brain, just like tuning an instrument to achieve perfect harmony. Antipsychotics dampen or block the effects of dopamine, a neurotransmitter often excessively active during manic episodes. It's akin to lowering the volume when the music becomes overwhelming, preventing the brain from becoming inundated. Antidepressants elevate serotonin and norepinephrine levels in the brain to enhance mood, analogous to adding sugar to coffee to sweeten it. Mood stabilizers are commonly used to manage conditions like Bipolar disorder by preventing extreme highs (mania) and lows (depression). These medications regulate certain chemicals in the brain, such as neurotransmitters, which play a role in controlling mood.

The key to successful medication use is not just about taking the medication; it's about finding the correct prescription and dosage. This often involves a trial-and-error process, which can be challenging. However, it's important to remember that it's a collaborative effort between you and your doctor. Clear communication is crucial to achieve the perfect biochemical equilibrium. You shouldn't feel drugged when you find the right combination; you should feel more like your usual self. These medications will not change who you are.

This collaborative approach reassures you that you are not alone in this journey.

3.2 Navigating Side Effects

Vigilance is crucial when it comes to side effects. These can range from minor inconveniences to significant concerns necessitating dosage adjustments or medication changes. It is recommended you read the literature on your particular prescription. Ensure your doctor knows all medications you're taking to mitigate interactions and minimize side effects. Many medications have been around since the mid-1950s, and their effects and side effects have been well-documented. These are referred to as 'typical' or first-generation medications. In the 90s, new medications were developed and are referred to as second-generation or 'atypical' medications. A common concern among antipsychotic medications is Tardive Dyskinesia (TD), which causes involuntary muscle movements. This can be controlled with an additional pill or by reducing dosage. Being proactive about side effects can help you manage your health more effectively.

One last caution on side effects: Like many other things in our bodies, these medications are metabolized by the liver or the kidneys; therefore, it is wise to have your doctor monitor both liver and kidney functions as necessary.

3.3 Understanding Medication Options

Numerous resources offer guidance through the plethora of medication options. Don't be daunted by terms like antipsychotics, anticonvulsants, reuptake inhibitors, or all the acronyms; many medications target multiple areas of the brain and neurotransmitter chemicals. Our understanding of how some medications work is limited, reflecting the vast gaps in our knowledge of the brain. Only recently have we been able to measure the levels of neurotransmitters in the brain to some extent. With just that bit of progress, we have been able to determine that the term 'chemical imbalance' is a misnomer because, in fact, there is no noticeable reduction of serotonin in depression. However, the term helps clarify and visualize the reason for the disease.

Another example of unintentional effects of drugs is that some diabetes management medications are now being used on non-diabetics for weight loss. Once the effects are observed, the medication goes through a process to see if it can be approved for the alternate treatment. Discussing how the brain works may help you further navigate this maze. However, it is a little far from the scope of this book because I promised no overtechnical medical jargon. But I can refer you to Ashley L. Peterson's "Psych Meds Made Simple." She does a beautiful job explaining neurotransmitters, receptors, regions of the brain, and what they have to do with our illnesses.

To give a general idea, below is a list of some of the naturally occurring chemicals in humans:

- **Serotonin**: Regulates mood, appetite, sleep, and memory. Imbalances in serotonin levels are associated with mood disorders like depression and anxiety.

- **Dopamine**: Plays a role in motivation, pleasure, reward, and movement control. It is involved in addiction, attention, and mood regulation.

- **Epinephrine (adrenaline)**: A neurotransmitter and stress hormone that plays a role in attention, alertness, and the body's fight-or-flight response.

- **Acetylcholine**: Involved in muscle movement, learning, memory, and attention and in regulating the autonomic nervous system.

- **Gamma-aminobutyric acid (GABA)**: An inhibitory neurotransmitter that helps reduce neuronal excitability. It is involved in relaxation, sleep, and anxiety regulation.

- **Glutamate**: Functions as the primary excitatory neurotransmitter in the brain, playing a role in learning, memory, and synaptic plasticity.

- **Endorphins**: Act as natural painkillers and are involved in the body's response to stress and exercise. They also contribute to feelings of pleasure and euphoria.

3.4 Addressing Common Misconceptions

One common misconception is that psychiatric medications are a crutch for the weak or that they fundamentally alter who you are. This stigma can prevent people from seeking the help they need. It's necessary to recognize that mental health conditions are as real and as debilitating as physical illnesses. Just as you wouldn't tell someone with diabetes to forgo insulin, it's unreasonable to suggest that someone with a mental health disorder should avoid medication. These medications do not change your personality or who you are; they help you manage your condition so you can be yourself.

Another myth is that medications are a quick fix. In reality, finding the proper medication and dosage is often a lengthy process involving careful monitoring and adjustments. This trial-and-error approach can be frustrating, but it's essential for finding the most effective treatment with the fewest side effects. Patience, persistence, and open communication with your healthcare provider are key to successful treatment.

There's also a belief that natural or holistic remedies are always better than pharmaceuticals. While lifestyle changes, therapy, and holistic approaches can be beneficial, they are not always sufficient on their own. Medications can play a crucial role in managing symptoms that other treatments might not fully address. It's not a matter of choosing one over the other but finding a balanced approach that works for you.

In conclusion, psychiatric medications are an essential tool in the treatment of mental health disorders. They help restore balance to the brain's chemistry, enabling individuals to lead more stable and fulfilling lives. Misconceptions about these medications can prevent people from seeking the help they need but understanding how they work and the role they play in managing mental health can dispel these myths. Remember, the journey to finding the correct medication is a collaborative effort between you and your doctor, and it's a process that requires patience, vigilance, and open communication. By being informed and proactive about your treatment, you can take control of your mental health and improve your quality of life.

3.5 Newer Treatment Modalities

Recent advancements in psychiatric treatment are expanding beyond traditional medications:

- **Third-Generation Antipsychotics**: Drugs like aripiprazole (Abilify) and brexpiprazole (Rexulti) offer different mechanisms of action and improved side effect profiles compared to earlier antipsychotics.

- **Long-Acting Injectables (LAIs)**: These are used for conditions like schizophrenia and bipolar disorder, providing medication that lasts for weeks or months, improving adherence and outcomes.

- **Ketamine and Esketamine**: These newer treatments for depression work rapidly, within hours or days, unlike traditional antidepressants that can take weeks to become effective. Esketamine, delivered as a nasal spray, has been particularly promising for treatment-resistant depression.

3.6 Pharmacogenomics

Pharmacogenomics is an emerging field that studies how an individual's genetic makeup affects their drug response. This has significant implications for psychiatric medications:

- **Personalized Medicine**: By analyzing a patient's genetic profile, doctors can better predict which medications and dosages will be most effective and have the fewest side effects. This personalized approach reduces the trial-and-error process of finding the proper medication.

3.7 Non-Traditional Medications

Some medications not traditionally used for psychiatric conditions are finding new roles in mental health treatment:

- **Antihypertensives**: Drugs like propranolol, a beta-blocker, are used off-label to manage anxiety and PTSD symptoms due to their effects on physical anxiety symptoms.

- **Anticonvulsants**: Medications like lamotrigine and valproate, initially developed for epilepsy, are now commonly used as mood stabilizers in bipolar disorder.

3.8 Off-Label Use

Off-label use of medications is common in psychiatry. This refers to prescribing drugs for conditions outside their approved indications:

- **Examples**: Clonidine, approved for hypertension, is often used to treat ADHD and anxiety. Similarly, antipsychotics like quetiapine are sometimes used off-label for insomnia due to their sedative properties.

The Future of Psychiatric Medications

Looking ahead, the future of psychiatric medications holds promise with ongoing research and development:

- **Neurostimulation**: Techniques like transcranial magnetic stimulation (TMS) and deep brain stimulation (DBS) are being explored as alternatives or adjuncts to medication for treatment-resistant conditions.

- **New Mechanisms**: Research into new neurotransmitter systems and pathways is ongoing, potentially leading to novel medications with unique mechanisms of action and better side effect profiles.

Treatment Strategies and Management

Welcome to the wild world of managing bipolar disorder, where the right combination of tools, tricks, and treatments can sometimes feel like you're trying to solve a Rubik's Cube blindfolded. But fear not! This chapter is about demystifying one of the most crucial aspects of that puzzle: medications. Think of it as your guide to the pharmacy aisle, except instead of finding the best deal on shampoo, you're navigating through mood stabilizers, antipsychotics, and antidepressants. Exciting, right? Let's dive in without tripping over medical jargon and maybe even have a few laughs.

4.1 Understanding Medication Options

Navigating the medication tangle in Bipolar disorder can be a bit like finding your way through a carnival funhouse—distorted mirrors and all. Several medications are commonly prescribed, each playing a different role in balancing the brain's biochemistry. First up, we have mood stabilizers. These are the heavy lifters, helping to even out the highs of mania and the lows of depression. Think of them as your emotional shock absorbers, smoothing those bumpy neurological roads.

Next, we introduce the antipsychotics. Despite their somewhat intimidating name, these medications are like the bouncers at the club of your brain. They help manage severe symptoms of mania and also help with psychotic symptoms, which can include delusions or hallucinations, should those be part of your experience.

Last but not least, we have antidepressants. Typically used cautiously in bipolar disorder due to the risk of triggering manic episodes, they're like the person who brings you a hot cup of tea (or a strong coffee) when you're feeling down, helping lift the fog of depression.

Navigating this medley of medications isn't about popping pills willy-nilly but finding a tailored blend that works for your unique brain chemistry. It's a bit like being a DJ mixing tracks—you need to find the right balance so the beat goes on smoothly without any unexpected drops. We will cover more about medications in the next chapter.

Medication Adherence

Sticking to your medication plan is as crucial as the plan itself. But let's be honest; adding one more thing to your daily to-do list isn't always easy. Here's where strategies to keep you on track come in handy. Setting reminders on your phone, using a pill organizer, or aligning your medication times with daily routines like brushing your teeth can all help make adherence less of a chore. It's about weaving these habits into the fabric of your day until they become as automatic as checking your email.

Medication adherence is critical for the success of psychiatric treatment:

Challenges: Patients may struggle with adherence due to side effects, forgetfulness, or misunderstanding the importance of taking their medication consistently.

Strategies: Using pill organizers, setting reminders, and simplifying dosing schedules can help improve adherence. Long-acting injectables can also ensure consistent medication levels.

Remember, these medications are not just pills but pillars that support your mental architecture. Missing doses or stopping suddenly can not only diminish their effectiveness but also lead to withdrawal symptoms or relapse. It's like skipping a beat in a meticulously timed dance routine—it throws everything off.

Collaborating with Your Doctor

Lastly, let's talk about perfecting the art of collaboration with your doctor. Open communication about how the medication affects you, any side effects you're experiencing, and your concerns make a huge difference. It's like having a co-pilot in the cockpit; you're on the journey together, navigating through the clouds. Don't hesitate to ask questions or express concerns—your health, mind, and life are on the line.

Sharing detailed feedback with your doctor helps you tailor your treatment plan more effectively. Maybe a particular medication makes you feel too tired, or another isn't entirely taking the edge off depression. This feedback is invaluable. It helps your doctor adjust dosages or try new medications, ensuring that your treatment plan fits not just a diagnosis but you as an individual.

Navigating the world of medications for bipolar disorder is an indispensable element of your overall management strategy. It's about more than just swallowing pills; it's about understanding their role, sticking to your regimen, and working collaboratively with your healthcare provider to fine-tune your treatment. Whether you're a newbie just starting this journey or a seasoned traveler on the bipolar road, getting the medication mix right can make all the difference. So, take charge, stay informed, and open the lines of communication with your doctor. Your brain will thank you.

4.2 Psychotherapy and Bipolar: A Guide to Effective Therapy Options

When it comes to navigating the ups and downs of bipolar disorder, psychotherapy is like having a skilled navigator aboard your ship, helping you steer through stormy seas and sunny days alike. It's not just about talking; it's about transforming your approach to daily challenges, giving you the tools to manage your mood swings and maintain relationships. Let's break down the types of psychotherapy that often stand out in the treatment of bipolar disorder, each with its unique flavor and strengths.

Cognitive Behavioral Therapy (CBT) is like having a mental detective by your side, helping you to spot and change thought patterns that may lead you to emotional pitfalls. Focuses on changing unhelpful thought patterns and behaviors through cognitive restructuring and skill development. Think of it as mental judo; you learn to leverage your thoughts in a way that helps you balance your mental state. It's convenient for tackling the negative thought spirals that can occur during depressive episodes or the unchecked optimism of manic phases. By recognizing these thoughts as symptoms of your disorder rather than truths, you can start to take control back from Bipolar disorder's grip.

Dialectical Behavior Therapy (DBT), on the other hand, emphasizes navigating emotional storms by teaching you to balance acceptance and change. It integrates mindfulness (being fully present in the moment), distress tolerance (getting through tough times without making them worse), emotional regulation (managing and responding to intense feelings effectively), and interpersonal effectiveness to help individuals manage intense emotions and improve relationships. Initially developed for borderline personality disorder, its usefulness in controlling the fierce emotional swings in bipolar disorder has gained recognition.

Family-focused therapy brings your support crew into the fold, training them alongside you in the skills needed to manage Bipolar disorder. It's about strengthening your support network by giving your loved ones the tools and understanding necessary to assist you. They learn about warning signs and the best response methods, which can make all the difference during a crisis or instability. Think of it as fortifying your home's foundations, ensuring everyone inside knows how to keep it stable.

Integrating therapy with medication creates a synergy that often leads to better outcomes. Imagine you are trying to cultivate a beautiful garden—medication helps to keep the weeds at bay while therapy nurtures the growth of healthy plants. Together, they ensure a more resilient and flourishing garden. Medication can stabilize your mood swings, making it easier to engage in therapy, while the skills and insights gained from therapy can help you make the most of your medication by sticking to your treatment plan and avoiding triggers that could lead to mood episodes.

Finding the right therapist is significant; it's like finding the right personal trainer for your mental health. You need someone who isn't just qualified but also someone you can click with, someone who gets it. Start by looking for therapists who specialize in bipolar disorder or mood disorders more broadly. They're more likely to understand the nuances of the condition and offer the most effective strategies. When you first meet, don't hesitate to ask about their experience and approach. Questions like, "How do you tailor your therapy to work with bipolar disorder?" or "Can you tell me about your experiences with other clients who have bipolar disorder?" can provide insights into their expertise and approach.

Don't forget to use resources such as psychologytoday.com, where you can filter therapists by specialty and insurance. Local support groups and your psychiatrist may also have recommendations. Remember, finding the right therapist might take time. It's like dating; you might not find the perfect match on the first try, but finding someone who can genuinely support your journey to stability is worth the effort.

In sum, psychotherapy offers a toolkit for living with bipolar disorder, not just by managing symptoms but by enriching your understanding of yourself and enhancing your relationships. Whether through CBT (Cognitive Behavioral Therapy), DBT (Dialectical Behavior Therapy), family-focused therapy, or another modality, therapy can be a cornerstone of effective bipolar disorder management, providing structure, support, and strategies for a fulfilling life despite the challenges of the condition.

4.3 Lifestyle Management: Diet, Exercise, and Sleep

Imagine that your body is like a finely tuned sports car; what you put into it and how you treat it can dictate how well it performs. For those navigating the winding roads of bipolar disorder, understanding the profound impact of diet, exercise, and sleep on your overall health isn't just good advice—it's crucial maintenance.

Diet and Nutrition

Let's start with fuel—your diet. Food is not just sustenance; it's information for your body and brain, and the right kinds can help stabilize your mood and enhance your energy levels. Think of your gut as a second brain, intricately linked to your actual brain. When your gut is happy and stocked with good fuel, it sends positive signals to your brain, potentially leading to more stable moods. So, what's on the menu for keeping both brains happy?

A bipolar-friendly diet leans heavily on the Mediterranean eating style—rich in vegetables, fruits, whole grains, fish, and olive oil. These foods are not just delicious; they are also packed with nutrients that can help combat the biological stress that often accompanies bipolar disorder. Omega-3 fatty acids found abundantly in fish like salmon and flaxseeds are particularly good at this. They're like your brain's best friends, helping to smooth out mood swings and protect against depression. On the other hand, try to steer clear of the villains—highly processed foods, excessive caffeine, and sugar. These can lead to mood crashes and throw your energy levels out of whack.

Incorporating these dietary changes doesn't have to be a chore or a bore. Spice it up; make it an adventure! Experiment with new recipes that include these brain-boosting foods. Maybe start a weekly tradition of cooking a new dish from a different culture that follows these guidelines. Not only are you feeding your body what it needs, but you're also breaking the monotony that sometimes comes with dietary restrictions.

Exercise as a Tool

Next up, let's talk about exercise. If diet is your car's fuel, exercise is the maintenance that keeps it running smoothly. Regular physical activity is a fantastic tool for managing bipolar disorder. It helps regulate mood, reduce stress, and improve sleep—trifecta! When you exercise, your brain releases endorphins, sometimes known as feel-good hormones. It's like giving your brain a mini-vacation.

The key here is regularity and enjoyment. Find activities that you actually enjoy. Hate running? No problem. How about dancing, hiking, or maybe a cycling class? The goal is to get moving, whatever that looks like for you. Aim for moderate intensity, and try to be consistent. Setting small, achievable goals, like a 30-minute walk five days a week, can make a big difference. It's not about training for a marathon (unless that's your thing) but about weaving movement into your day to keep your mood balanced.

The Importance of Sleep

Let's dim the lights and talk about sleep—your body's best regeneration tool. Sleep and bipolar disorder have a complex relationship. Poor sleep can trigger manic episodes or deepen depressive episodes, while stable sleep patterns tend to support mood stability. Developing good sleep hygiene is crucial. This means creating a bedtime routine that signals to your body it's time to wind down. Maybe it's a warm bath, turning off blue light-emitting devices an hour before bed, or reading a book chapter (preferably not a thriller!).

Keep your sleep and wake times consistent, even on weekends. This regularity trains your brain when to shut down for rest and stabilizes your internal clock, which can help manage your mood. Consider it setting your body's alarm system to protect against mood swings.

Integrating Lifestyle Changes

Finally, let's piece it all together. Integrating these changes into your daily routine might seem daunting at first. Start small. Introduce changes gradually, and celebrate the small victories. Maybe this week, you focus on improving your diet; next week, you add a few exercise routines; and the week after, you tighten up your sleep schedule. Small steps lead to significant changes.

Remember, managing bipolar disorder is a holistic journey. Your diet, exercise, and sleep are not just parts of a treatment plan—they are integral components of a healthy lifestyle. Each element supports the other, creating a synergy that can significantly enhance your ability to manage your mood and improve your overall quality of life. So, take the time to nourish your body, challenge it with physical activity, and rest it well. Your mind will thank you, and you might find yourself feeling more balanced and prepared to handle whatever twists and turns bipolar disorder throws your way.

4.4 The Impact of Stress and How to Manage It

Let's face it: Stress is as avoidable as reruns of old sitcoms on TV—it's always there, and sometimes it's mildly entertaining, but often, it just feels repetitive and exhausting. For those navigating the waves of bipolar disorder, stress isn't just a nuisance; it can be a significant trigger, turning what feels like a manageable day into an emotional upheaval. Understanding how stress interacts with bipolar disorder isn't just about keeping your sanity on a bad day; it's about equipping yourself with tools to keep the boat steady even when the weather turns foul.

Stress, in the context of bipolar disorder, can act like a spark in a pile of dry leaves. It can ignite manic or depressive episodes, making it not just an emotional response but a biochemical game-changer. This happens because stress hormones like cortisol can affect brain function, influencing mood, thinking, and even how you process other stimuli. It's like turning up the volume on your emotions; everything feels more intense, and suddenly, the coping mechanisms you usually rely on might not cut it. This is why embedding effective stress management techniques into your daily routine isn't just good practice; it's essential maintenance for your mental health.

So, how do you keep stress from steering the ship? First, recognize what your stressors are. These can be as obvious as a significant life change or as subtle as a poor night's sleep. Sometimes, writing these down can help you see patterns or triggers you weren't aware of. Next, arm yourself with a toolbox of stress reduction techniques. Relaxation exercises can be a good start. This isn't just about taking deep breaths or meditating, though those are excellent strategies. It's also about finding activities that distract your mind from stressors and give you a break. Maybe it's painting, playing an instrument, or even gardening— anything that helps you shift gears and allows your brain a moment to rest and reset.

Time management strategies also play a crucial role. Often, stress bubbles up from feeling like you're running out of time or not in control of your schedule. By prioritizing tasks, setting realistic goals, and breaking down your day into manageable chunks, you can reduce the chaos that often leads to stress. Think of it as decluttering your day; when each task has its place, and you know what to expect, the day feels less overwhelming.

Setting healthy boundaries is another strategic move. This means learning to say no or step back when overwhelmed. It's about recognizing your limits and communicating them to others. In a world that often praises the hustle, stepping off the treadmill and catching your breath is okay. Remember, saying no to others sometimes means saying yes to your well-being.

Creating a supportive, low-stress environment is like setting the stage for a smoother performance. At home, this might mean organizing your space to reduce chaos, using soothing colors or decor, and establishing a sanctuary where you can retreat when things get too hectic. At work, it might involve negotiating your workload or deadlines to suit your mental health needs better or setting up your workspace to minimize stress. Think about what changes can make your daily environments more calming and supportive, and don't hesitate to make those changes.

Long-term stress management is about building resilience. It's not just about handling stress as it comes but developing systems and habits that make you less susceptible to stress in the first place. Regular exercise, a consistent sleep schedule, and ongoing therapy or support groups can all contribute to a baseline of stability that makes you less likely to be knocked off balance when stress does hit. It's about fortifying your defenses, not just patching up leaks as they happen.

Incorporating these strategies into your life doesn't just help manage stress; it transforms how you interact with your world. It's about turning stress management from a fire-fighting tool into a blueprint for a more balanced, resilient life. By understanding the triggers, employing reduction techniques, and creating supportive environments, you're not just surviving with bipolar disorder; you're thriving despite it.

4.5 Holistic Approaches: Complementing Traditional Treatments

When you think about managing bipolar disorder, your mind might first wander to the usual suspects: medications and therapy. But imagine adding some more tools to your wellness toolkit—ones that might seem a bit unconventional but can harmonize beautifully with your standard care. I'm talking about holistic approaches like acupuncture, yoga, and meditation. These aren't just new-age fads; they're practices rooted in ancient traditions, now backed by modern science and gaining ground as valuable allies in managing bipolar disorder.

Let's start with acupuncture, a technique involving the insertion of very thin needles through your skin at strategic points on your body, a key component of traditional Chinese medicine. It's like having a secret map of energy points on your body, and when these points are activated, they can help recalibrate your body's energy flow or Qi. For those with bipolar disorder, acupuncture has been noted to help reduce stress and anxiety, potentially lessening the intensity of mood swings. Picture this as trying to smooth out waves before they become too turbulent. While the thought of needles might make some a bit squeamish, many report these sessions as surprisingly relaxing and rejuvenating.

Then, there's yoga, which is much more than just stretching and holding poses. It's a complete package of benefits wrapped in calm and centeredness. Yoga combines physical postures, breathing exercises, and meditation to enhance physical flexibility, mental clarity, and emotional stability. For someone managing Bipolar disorder, this trinity can be particularly potent. Engaging in yoga can be akin to tuning an instrument—aligning your body, mind, and emotions to play harmoniously. It's about building inner strength and flexibility, not just physically but also emotionally, providing a buffer against the strain of mood swings.

Meditation, the practice of mindfulness or focused thought, can be a profound tool for those with bipolar disorder. It's about sitting with your thoughts in a way that lets you observe them without becoming entangled. Over time, this practice can enhance your ability to monitor your mood and triggers more effectively, fostering a kind of mental agility that can be crucial in managing the disorder. Think of it as training your mind to be an observer, which can help you detach and assess rather than spiral in moments of high emotion or stress.

My personal favorite is Pilates. Pilates is a comprehensive fitness system with numerous benefits, including improved strength, flexibility, posture, and mental well-being. It's suitable for people of all ages and fitness levels and can be practiced in various settings, including gyms, studios, and even at home, with minimal equipment. It does not impact your joints, and focusing on breathing fully helps to center you.

While these practices offer promising benefits, it's crucial to incorporate them into your treatment plan with care and knowledge. Always consult with your healthcare provider before starting any new treatment regimen. They can help you integrate these holistic practices to support and enhance your treatment plan. For instance, combining meditation with medication might help you achieve better emotional balance, while yoga could complement therapy by reducing physical tension and mental stress that exacerbate symptoms.

Let's dive into some personal stories highlighting these holistic approaches' real-world impact. Consider Sarah, a long-time sufferer of bipolar II disorder, who found yoga not just a physical exercise but a lifeline. For her, yoga became a daily ritual that helped stabilize her mood and provided a sense of control over her body and mind. Then there's Mike, who explored acupuncture as an adjunct to his medication, only to discover that the sessions significantly reduced his anxiety, a common trigger for his depressive episodes. These stories underscore the potential of holistic practices to complement traditional treatments and enhance overall well-being.

Incorporating holistic approaches into your bipolar management strategy offers a broader canvas of options. It's about personalizing your treatment, mixing traditional and holistic tools to create a tailored approach that addresses your unique needs. Whether it's the calming flow of yoga, the centeredness of meditation, or the balancing touch of acupuncture or Pilates, each practice offers a pathway to greater harmony and health. Embrace these options with openness and curiosity, and you might find they add not only relief but also enrichment to your journey of managing bipolar disorder, painting a fuller picture of wellness that extends beyond conventional treatments.

4.6 Navigating Treatment Side Effects and Balance

When you first start your medication for bipolar disorder, it's like setting sail on a voyage across a vast ocean. The journey promises smoother seas, but sometimes, you must weather a few storms. Side effects from medications can be those storms—unpredictable and unsettling. Whether it's a queasy stomach from your mood stabilizers, a drowsy fog from your antipsychotics, or a case of the jitters from your antidepressants, side effects are often the crew members on your medication ship that you didn't realize you hired.

Common side effects can vary widely, but they often include nausea, weight gain, dizziness, or sleep disturbances. Imagine you're at a buffet where you're served a platter of unwanted side dishes instead of picking dishes that tantalize your taste buds. It's crucial not to push these around your plate but to find ways to manage them effectively. Simple strategies might involve adjusting the timing of when you take your meds—perhaps taking them with food to ease nausea or switching to evening doses to counter drowsiness. Sometimes, it's about adding a little something extra to your daily routine, like a morning walk or an additional glass of water, to counterbalance the side effects you're experiencing. Most of these side effects taper off after two weeks, others a little longer. I suffer from tremors. My solution was to step down the dosage of my mood stabilizer.

Knowing when to speak up about side effects is like knowing when to call in a lifeline during a game show. You don't have to struggle silently, guessing at solutions. Open communication with your healthcare provider is required. They're like your co-navigators; let them know what's going on. Many side effects can be managed with adjustments to your treatment plan, including tweaking dosages, switching medications, or adding remedies to counteract specific side effects. It's like adjusting your sails to the wind; sometimes, a slight shift can significantly affect how smoothly you sail.

Balancing the benefits of treatment with its side effects is a bit like being a judge at a talent show; you have to weigh the performances (benefits) against the stage mishaps (side effects). It's essential to consider how the treatment improves your quality of life. Is the mood stabilization worth the extra pounds? Does the clarity brought by antidepressants justify feeling a bit jittery? These are personal decisions; sometimes, they're tough calls. It's about looking at your life and deciding what's most important for your well-being. Remember, the goal of treatment is not just to reduce symptoms of bipolar disorder but to enhance your overall quality of life.

Empowering yourself to advocate in your treatment discussions is like stepping up to the captain's deck of your ship. You know the waters best. If something doesn't feel right or the side effects overshadow the benefits, it's your right and responsibility to speak up. Prepare for appointments with notes on what you've experienced, do your research, and don't be shy about asking for adjustments. It's about having a dialogue, not a monologue, with your healthcare provider. Make your voice heard, and ensure your treatment plan is a true collaboration tailored to your needs.

Navigating treatment side effects is an integral part of managing bipolar disorder. It requires awareness, communication, and, sometimes, a bit of creativity. By understanding common side effects, speaking up, balancing benefits with drawbacks, and advocating for yourself, you can find a treatment balance that manages your symptoms and supports a well-lived life. Remember, it's not just about weathering storms but about enjoying the journey, and with the right strategies, you can continue to steer towards clearer skies.

As we close this chapter on navigating treatment side effects, remember that the journey with bipolar disorder is both complex and manageable. Each step you take—adjusting medications, communicating with your doctor, or advocating for your needs— builds a stronger foundation for your ongoing management. These strategies are crucial, not just for handling the challenges of today but for paving the way to a more stable and fulfilling tomorrow. As you continue to navigate these waters, know that each effort contributes to a broader journey towards wellness, one where balance isn't just possible but achievable. Stay the course, adjust as necessary, and keep your sights on the horizon of your best life. Now, let's sail onward to exploring further dimensions of living with Bipolar disorder in the next chapter.

Daily Life Adjustments and Coping Strategies

Have you ever felt like you're trying to juggle flaming torches while riding a unicycle on a tightrope? Well, managing daily life with bipolar disorder can sometimes feel a bit like that—exciting, unpredictable, and, yes, a tad overwhelming. But here's the good news: incorporating structured routines into your day can be like having a safety net below that tightrope, providing stability and confidence as you navigate your day. This chapter is about turning those flaming torches into manageable juggling balls and, perhaps, with some practice, making that unicycle ride a smooth sail.

5.1 Routine as a Rescue: Structuring Your Day for Stability

Benefits of a Routine

Imagine your daily routine as the rhythm section of a band—it might not always be the flashiest part, but boy, does it keep the music flowing smoothly! For those with bipolar disorder, a well-structured routine can be a lifesaver. It provides a predictable and familiar pattern that can help soothe the brain, reducing the likelihood of manic or depressive episodes. This doesn't just apply to big things like work or appointments; it includes little things like eating, exercising, or sleeping before bed.

Consistency is key. By waking up, taking medications, working, and sleeping regularly, you create a rhythm your body and mind can tune with. It's like setting the tempo for your daily life symphony—too fast, and the music gets chaotic, too slow, and it drags. But just right? Harmony. This regularity helps regulate your body's internal clock, or circadian rhythm, which is crucial in managing mood swings. Think of it as teaching your body to expect what's next, which can be incredibly comforting in a world that often feels like it's spinning a little too fast.

Creating a Personalized Routine

But here's the twist: while routines are great, they aren't one-size-fits-all. Your routine must be tailored to fit your life, needs, and, yes, your quirks. Start by mapping out a typical day, noting the must-dos and the want-to-dos. Include time slots for non-negotiables, like taking medication or attending therapy sessions. Then, weave in activities that bring you joy or provide relaxation. Do you love to read? Set aside 30 minutes before bed as your designated reading time. Is coffee your morning ritual? Build that into your morning routine as something to savor, not just gulp down.

Use tools that help you stick to this routine. Apps that remind you to take your meds, calendars ping you about appointments, or even a good old-fashioned planner can help keep you on track. The goal is to build a routine that doesn't feel like a straitjacket but rather like your favorite cozy sweater—comforting, reliable, and snugly fitting into your life.

Flexibility Within Structure

However, life is nothing if not a series of unexpected events. While a routine provides structure, being too rigid can actually create stress, which is counterproductive. It's essential to build flexibility into your routine. For instance, if you've planned to go to the gym in the morning but wake up feeling sluggish and out of sorts, it might be better to adjust your schedule and go for a gentle walk in the evening instead.

Think of your routine as a guideline, not a rule book. Life will throw curve balls—sick days, surprise visits, work crises—and your routine should be resilient enough to handle these. This flexibility reduces stress and empowers you to make choices that best suit your needs at any given moment, fostering a sense of control and self-efficacy.

Examples of Successful Routines

Let's draw some inspiration from others who've mastered the art of the routine. Take Julia, for example, a freelance graphic designer who balances her projects with managing bipolar II disorder. Her mornings begin with meditation and a light workout, which she says "kicks off my day on a positive note." Work follows, but she breaks every hour for five minutes to stretch or do breathing exercises, keeping stress levels in check. Evenings are for relaxation—reading, cooking, or photography.

Then there's Michael, a high school teacher, who finds stability in the very structure of his job. His weekdays are rigorously scheduled with teaching, planning, and grading, but he reserves his evenings for quiet time with his family, which he calls his "daily dose of happiness." Weekends are less structured to allow for spontaneity, giving him a balance between routine and relaxation.

These examples underscore that while the specifics of a routine will vary, the essence remains the same: a blend of structure and flexibility that supports both the management of bipolar disorder and the pursuit of personal fulfillment. Remember, the goal of a routine isn't to confine you but to liberate you, providing a framework within which you can live more freely and fully, even amidst the ups and downs of bipolar disorder. So, take these ideas, tailor them to your life, and start building your own rhythm that makes your daily symphony more harmonious.

5.2 Mindfulness and Meditation: Tools for Emotional Regulation

Let's talk about mindfulness and meditation—two buzzwords you've probably heard tossed around like confetti at a New Year's party. But beyond the hype, these practices are like secret weapons for anyone grappling with the emotional roller coaster of Bipolar disorder. Mindfulness isn't just a trendy practice; it's about anchoring yourself in the present moment, which can be a game-changer when your emotions seem determined to throw you off balance.

Imagine you're a surfer. Each wave represents a different emotion or thought. Mindfulness teaches you to ride these waves without getting pulled under by the current of your thoughts or moods. It's about observing these waves—acknowledging their presence without letting them dictate where you go. This kind of emotional regulation is crucial in bipolar disorder, where your mood can shift dramatically and sometimes unpredictably. Practicing mindfulness can increase awareness of these shifts, often gaining precious moments to make informed decisions rather than being swept away.

Incorporating mindfulness into your daily life doesn't require sitting cross-legged for hours or chanting mantras—unless that's your jam. It can be as simple as taking a mindful walk. Try to notice each step the next time you walk to your mailbox or around the neighborhood. Feel your foot as it meets the ground, the rhythm of your breath, the sounds around you. This isn't just about enjoying a walk; it's about training your mind to stay focused on the present, which can significantly reduce stress and anxiety.

Now, let's dial into meditation. If mindfulness is about staying present during your daily activities, meditation is the workout session for your mind. It strengthens your ability to concentrate and calm your mind. Starting a meditation practice can be as simple as dedicating five minutes daily to sit quietly and focus on your breath. When thoughts intrude—and they will—gently acknowledge them and then bring your focus back to your breathing. Over time, these few minutes can expand, and the calmness and focus you cultivate during these sessions can spill over into the rest of your day.

Ample resources exist for those wondering how to deepen their practice or learn more about integrating these tools into their life. Apps like Headspace or Calm offer guided meditations and are perfect for beginners. They take you through the basics and gradually help you build a meditation practice that can withstand the busyness of modern life. Books like "Wherever You Go, There You Are" by Jon Kabat-Zinn can provide deeper insights into mindfulness, enriching your understanding and practice. For those who prefer a more structured learning environment, local community centers or wellness clinics often offer courses in mindfulness and meditation, providing guided instruction and community support.

Tapping into mindfulness and meditation opens up a new way to handle the complexities of Bipolar disorder, offering tools that enhance stability, promote mental clarity, and foster a greater sense of peace. You're surviving and thriving by incorporating these practices into your life—riding the waves with skill, grace, and resilience. So why not give it a try? Start small, stay consistent, and watch how these ancient practices can bring modern benefits to your life, transforming challenges into opportunities for growth and self-discovery.

5.3 Building a Support Network: Finding and Nurturing Relationships

Think of your support network as your personal cheerleading squad, emergency response team, and wisdom council all rolled into one. When you're dealing with bipolar disorder, these are the folks who will pass you tissues, share a laugh, or give that sage piece of advice when you need it most. The importance of this network can't be overstressed—it's a core part of not just surviving with bipolar disorder but genuinely thriving.

First off, let's chat about why a robust support network is such a big deal. Imagine you're trying to lift a heavy box. Doing it alone could be challenging, maybe even risky. But with a team, not only is the load lighter, but it's also less likely to drop on your toes. Similarly, a support network lightens the emotional and practical burdens of bipolar disorder. During a manic phase, they can help keep your feet on the ground. In a depressive episode, they're there to lift you up. And on the days when you're feeling just fine, they're there to share in the joy. It's about having a safety net and a sounding board, ensuring you're supported, no matter what the bipolar skies look like.

Now, identifying who makes it into your support squad is crucial. Not everyone will understand what you're going through, and that's okay. Start with those who've shown empathy and patience and were calm in previous storms. These might be friends, family members, or even coworkers. The key is their ability to provide support without judgment. A good litmus test is to think about how you feel after spending time with them. They might not fit your support network best if you leave feeling drained or anxious. But you're on the right track if you feel uplifted, understood, or simply calm.

But it's not just about who is already in your life. Sometimes, expanding your network can bring new perspectives and understanding. This is where support groups and online communities come into play. These groups are like finding a whole tribe of people who get it because they're walking similar paths. They can be invaluable sources of advice, empathy, and understanding. Whether it's a local meetup or an online forum, these communities can make you feel less alone in your struggles. They provide a platform to share experiences and tips and sometimes to vent in a space where others instinctively understand the highs and lows.

Maintaining these relationships is where the real work comes in. It's not just about having people around; it's about nurturing those connections. Communication is your best tool here. Be open about what you're experiencing and what kind of support you need. It might be someone to accompany you to a doctor's appointment, help with daily tasks when you're low, or simply a friend to call when you need to talk. Setting clear boundaries is also part of this communication. Let your support network know what is helpful and what is not, and be open to hearing their needs, too. Remember, these relationships are a two-way street. Just as you need support, you also need to be supportive.

Consider also the power of gratitude in these relationships. A simple thank you, a note, or a small gesture to show appreciation can go a long way in keeping the bonds strong. It's about showing that you value their support and reciprocating in ways that strengthen the relationship.

Building and maintaining a support network is like tending a garden. It takes patience, effort, and care, but the blooms that result can brighten even the darkest days. These relationships provide a buffer against the storms of bipolar disorder, offering light, warmth, and shelter. By investing in this network, you're not just creating a safety net but also enriching your life, making each day a little easier, brighter, and more connected.

5.4 Workplace Strategies: Thriving Professionally

When it comes to managing bipolar disorder in the professional arena, think of it as orchestrating a well-timed dance between your personal needs and your professional responsibilities. The workplace can either be a stage for triumphs or a battleground for challenges, and much of that depends on how you navigate the complexities of disclosure, accommodations, stress management, and career development. Let's unpack these elements, ensuring you're equipped to survive in your career and thrive.

Disclosure and Privacy

Deciding whether to disclose your bipolar disorder at work is akin to choosing whether to share a personal secret with a colleague—it can strengthen your connection and lead to support, or it can change dynamics in unpredictable ways. It's a highly personal decision, often influenced by your workplace environment, the nature of your job, and the severity of your symptoms. If your bipolar disorder significantly affects your job performance, disclosing it might be necessary to seek accommodations. However, this comes with considerations for privacy and the potential for stigma.

Navigating this decision requires understanding your legal protections. In many places, laws like the Americans with Disabilities Act (ADA) in the U.S. protect employees from discrimination based on disability and require employers to provide reasonable accommodations. However, these protections only kick in once a condition is disclosed officially. It's wise to weigh the benefits of potential support against the risks of possible stigma or misunderstanding. If you choose to disclose, consider doing so in a structured way—perhaps during a meeting with your HR representative, where you can discuss your condition and how it might be effectively managed at work. This approach protects your privacy while setting a professional tone for the conversation.

Accommodations for Bipolar Disorder

Once disclosure is out of the way, the next step is to consider what accommodations might help you manage your Bipolar disorder while maintaining your productivity. Accommodations can vary widely depending on your specific needs and the nature of your job. They might include flexible scheduling to attend doctor's appointments, the ability to work from home on days when symptoms are particularly challenging, or adjustments to your workspace to reduce stress and distractions.

For example, if you find that a noisy office environment triggers anxiety or makes it difficult to concentrate during depressive episodes, requesting a quieter workspace or noise-canceling headphones could be reasonable accommodations. Similarly, if sleep disruptions associated with your condition leave you drained, a flexible start time could help you manage your health without compromising your work responsibilities. The key is identifying which aspects of your job interact with your symptoms and seeking accommodations that directly address these intersections, facilitating a balance that supports your health and professional performance.

Managing Stress at Work

Stress management in the workplace is crucial since high stress can exacerbate bipolar symptoms, potentially leading to a cycle of mood instability and decreased productivity. Developing effective stress management techniques can be your shield against such cycles. Simple strategies like organized task management—using tools like digital calendars or to-do list apps—can help keep you on track without feeling overwhelmed. Regular breaks are also essential; a few minutes away from your desk to breathe deeply or stretch can significantly reduce stress levels.

Moreover, establishing clear boundaries around work hours and responsibilities can prevent the kind of overcommitment that leads to burnout. It's important to communicate openly with your supervisor about your workload and to advocate for a balance that supports your well-being. Remember, being proactive about stress management helps maintain stability and enhances your overall effectiveness and job satisfaction.

Career Development

Finally, managing bipolar disorder doesn't mean putting your professional aspirations on hold. It's entirely possible to advance your career and achieve your goals. This might involve seeking roles with a better work-life balance, pursuing further education to expand your qualifications, or finding a mentor who understands your unique challenges and can provide guidance and support.

Career development can also mean learning to leverage your strengths. Many individuals with bipolar disorder find that they are exceptionally creative, empathetic, or driven—traits that can be significant assets in many professional contexts. By focusing on roles that capitalize on these strengths, you can manage your condition more effectively and excel in your chosen field.

In navigating these professional waters, remember that managing bipolar disorder at work is not just about overcoming challenges; it's about leveraging your full potential, advocating for your needs, and building a fulfilling career that acknowledges and supports your mental health. With the right strategies, you can thrive professionally, not despite your bipolar disorder but in conjunction with managing it effectively.

5.5 Financial Management: Planning and Stability

Navigating the financial waters when you've got bipolar disorder riding shotgun can sometimes feel like trying to budget for a road trip without knowing the distance or the cost of gas. Especially when you factor in the price of treatments and the possibility of income fluctuations during episodes, having a sound financial plan isn't just helpful—it's crucial. It's about more than keeping your bank account in the green; it's about reducing financial stress that could worsen symptoms.

So, how do you start? Think of financial planning as building a dam to keep your resources flowing steadily, even when the weather changes unexpectedly. The first step is understanding the full scope of potential costs associated with bipolar disorder. These could range from medications and therapy sessions to possible hospital stays. It's a lot, but don't let it overwhelm you. Instead, break it down into manageable chunks. Start by listing these expenses and then assess your health insurance coverage. What's covered, what's not, and where might you need additional help? This clarity can be incredibly empowering and can prevent nasty surprises down the road.

Next up, let's talk budgeting—your financial road map. A budget accommodating your medical needs and regular expenses can help you avoid financial strain. Start by tracking your income and expenses for a month or two. See where your money is going, and identify areas where you can cut back without sacrificing your well-being. There are plenty of budgeting tools and apps out there that can make this process easier. Apps like Mint or YNAB (You Need A Budget) link to your financial accounts and automatically categorize your spending, making it easier to stick to your budget and spot trends over time.

Let's address the elephant in the room—impulsive spending during manic episodes. This cannot be easy when you are browsing at 3 am. It's like being on a shopping spree with a blindfold. To curb this, set up safeguards. One strategy might be to have a trusted friend or family member keep an eye on your spending. Some even go as far as arranging with their bank to require dual authorization for purchases above a certain amount during these phases. It's about creating a safety net that respects your independence while protecting you from potential financial harm.

Financial assistance resources are another critical piece of the puzzle. Many are unaware of the programs available to help manage the costs of medication and therapy. Pharmaceutical companies often offer patient assistance programs for medications, providing them at a lower price or even free to those who qualify. Websites like NeedyMeds provide information on such programs. Moreover, for therapy costs, organizations like the National Alliance on Mental Illness (NAMI) and local mental health clinics often offer resources or sliding-scale payment options based on income. Don't hesitate to reach out to these resources; they can provide a financial breather, allowing you to focus more on managing your health and less on managing your wallet.

Incorporating these financial management strategies into your life can create a buffer against the economic uncertainties of living with bipolar disorder. By taking control of your finances through careful planning, budgeting, and utilizing available resources, you not only safeguard your financial well-being but also reduce a significant source of stress, making your path a little smoother. And in a world that often feels like it's spinning a bit too fast, having that extra stability can make all the difference. So, take the wheel, set your course, and let's navigate these financial waters together, ensuring that you stay afloat even when the tides try to pull you under.

5.6 Creativity and Hobbies: Channeling Energy Positively

Let's paint a colorful picture here—imagine your creativity as a vibrant palette of paints, each shade representing a different aspect of your personality and potential. For those living with bipolar disorder, engaging in creative activities isn't just a way to pass the time; it's a form of therapy, a means of self-expression, and a powerful tool for managing the emotional spectrum that comes with the condition. Whether it's art, writing, music, or digging your hands into the earth of your garden, these activities offer more than just distraction—they provide a channel for turbulent and serene emotions. As I mentioned earlier, I'm not an artist, but art in the context of therapy is not about the quality of the art but about expressing yourself and letting the process of creating be like unpacking a suitcase full of things you didn't even know were there.

Think of times when manic energy feels like an electrical storm inside you. It's intense, buzzing, seemingly uncontainable. Now, imagine channeling that energy into painting a canvas, composing a piece of music, or writing a story. These creative outlets allow you to 'plug-in' that surging energy and transform it into something beautiful or at least meaningful. It's not about suppressing what you feel but redirecting it into something that doesn't just consume you but contributes to your world. The therapeutic benefits of these activities are well-documented. They can elevate your mood, decrease anxiety, and provide a sense of accomplishment and self-worth that are invaluable on days when the disorder tries to convince you otherwise.

Incorporating these hobbies and creative pursuits into your daily routine isn't about filling every spare minute with activity to ward off potential mood swings. It's about balance and fulfillment. Establishing a routine that includes time set aside for creativity can act as a stabilizing force. It creates a predictable, safe space each day for self-expression. This scheduled creativity time becomes a ritual, a checkpoint, a familiar friend that waits for you regardless of the day you're having. It's comforting to know that no matter the storm, there's a harbor where you can anchor, focus, and channel your thoughts and emotions in a productive, stabilizing way.

Take Vincent van Gogh, Sylvia Plath, Virginia Woolf, Frida Kahlo, etc. These well-known artists created some of their most iconic works while battling various mental illnesses. These are just a few examples, but countless other artists have channeled their struggles with mental illness into their creative work, producing deeply personal, emotionally resonant, and persistently influential art.

Now, let's draw inspiration from those who have turned their bipolar disorder into a driving force for their creativity, achieving significant accomplishments along the way. Take the example of a renowned author who channels her manic energy into writing novels, her rapid thoughts and boundless energy fueling her vibrant narratives. Or consider a musician whose deepest, most resonant songs were composed in the depths of a depressive phase, capturing emotions that strike a chord with others. These stories aren't just individual successes; they're beacons of possibility, showing that the energy and perspective of bipolar disorder can be powerful catalysts for creative achievement.

These narratives are important. They shift the story from one of struggle to one of potential. They show that while bipolar disorder is undoubtedly a challenging companion, it can also be a dynamic, creative ally if channeled appropriately. So, whether you're sketching in a notepad, strumming a guitar, or crafting poetry, remember these are more than hobbies; they are tools in your wellness kit, ways to balance your life, and channels to turn your experiences into art, insight, or simply, a release.

As this chapter closes, remember that integrating creativity and hobbies into your life is not just about managing bipolar disorder; it's about enriching your entire existence. These activities provide a unique way to balance your emotional world, offering both stability and a source of deep, personal fulfillment. They allow you to gracefully navigate the highs and lows, using the very energy of your symptoms to fuel your creative fire. Keep this canvas of opportunity ready, and paint your journey with the broad strokes of persistence, the detailed touches of self-awareness, and the vibrant colors of creativity. As we turn the page, let's carry forward this creative spirit, exploring further how personal growth and transformation are not just possible but within reach, even as we continue to manage and thrive with bipolar disorder.

Navigating Relationships and Bipolar

Try explaining to someone why you rearranged your entire living room at 3 AM, wearing the same superhero costume for a week straight...or disappearing for three days. It sounds like a quirky sitcom plot, right? But when you have bipolar disorder, these scenarios can be real life and not always as humorous to explain to loved ones. Navigating relationships when you have bipolar disorder is a bit like being a translator, constantly trying to translate your feelings and actions into a language that your loved ones can understand. This chapter dives into the ocean of relationship dynamics, fishing out the best communication strategies and showing you how to maintain a healthy social fleet, even when the bipolar seas get choppy.

6.1 Communication is Key: Talking About Bipolar with Loved Ones

The Role of Open Dialogue

Open dialogue about your bipolar disorder isn't just about keeping people informed; it's about letting them in. It's about turning what could be a monologue of internal struggles into a dialogue of shared understanding and support. Think of it like opening the doors to a secret garden – you're allowing someone to step into a part of your world that's intensely personal. This isn't just beneficial; it's transformative. It transforms isolation into intimacy and misconceptions into mutual understanding. By talking openly about your bipolar disorder, you're not just seeking sympathy but forging empathy, which is a far stronger foundation for any relationship.

But why is this so crucial? Because bipolar disorder doesn't just affect you. It ripples out, touching everyone in your life in some way. When those closest to you understand what you're going through, they're better equipped to offer the proper support when needed. They can recognize the signs that you're entering a manic or depressive phase before you do and can gently help steer you back, akin to a co-pilot helping to navigate through turbulent weather.

Effective Communication Techniques

Now, let's talk tactics. Effective communication about your bipolar disorder doesn't mean just blurting out everything during a family dinner—timing, tone, and transparency matter. Start by choosing a good time when you and your loved one are relaxed and there's enough time to dig deep. Use "I" statements, such as "I feel..." or "I experience..." to keep the conversation subjective and non-accusatory. This helps keep defenses down and empathy up.

It's also helpful to be as specific as possible about what bipolar disorder means for you. Everyone's experience with bipolar disorder is unique. Describe your symptoms, your triggers, and what adequate support looks like for you. Maybe bring a cheat sheet — a list of bullet points to ensure you cover the essentials without getting overwhelmed or sidetracked.

Setting Boundaries

While we're unpacking the communication toolkit, let's talk about boundaries. Setting healthy boundaries is like drawing a clear map of where you end and others begin. It's crucial because it protects your energy and emotions, preventing relationships from becoming draining or one-sided. Clear boundaries might look like saying no to social events when you're feeling low or asking for space during high-anxiety periods. It's not about building walls; it's about installing gates where needed, gates you can open when you choose.

And remember, setting boundaries is a two-way street. Just as you need your boundaries respected, you should respect the boundaries of others. This mutual respect creates a balanced relationship where both parties feel safe and valued.

Navigating Misunderstandings

Finally, let's tackle the big one: misunderstandings. They're inevitable, like rain at a picnic. Misunderstandings can stem from a lack of information, differences in perspective, or the unpredictable nature of bipolar disorder itself. When these occur, it's like hitting a pothole on the road; it can jolt you, but it doesn't have to derail the journey.

When a misunderstanding arises, address it directly and calmly. Re-explain your perspective if needed, and be open to hearing theirs. Sometimes, just acknowledging that bipolar disorder can make things confusing for everyone helps. Having a previously agreed-upon plan for handling conflicts is also beneficial, like taking a time-out to cool down or using a safe word when things get too heated.

Navigating relationships with bipolar disorder is no small feat, but with open communication, effective techniques, clear boundaries, and strategies for handling misunderstandings, you can maintain and even strengthen your connections. It's about turning challenges into opportunities for growth, understanding, and deeper bonding. And isn't that what relationships are all about? Growing together, understanding each other, and strengthening bonds? So, let's keep the dialogue open, the boundaries clear, and the understanding deep. With these tools, you're well-equipped to maintain healthy, supportive relationships, no matter how choppy the bipolar seas might get.

6.2 When Bipolar Strains Relationships: Coping Strategies for Couples

Navigating a romantic relationship can often feel like dancing a delicate tango, where every step and turn must be in sync. Throw bipolar disorder into the mix, and that dance can sometimes feel more like a mosh pit at a rock concert, where unpredictability is the only expectation. The truth is that bipolar disorder introduces a set of challenges that can test the strongest of partnerships. It can stretch the fabric of intimacy, twist the dynamics of interaction, and add an intense strain on both partners. Recognizing these challenges is the first step towards managing them, not just for the sake of maintaining the relationship but for nurturing it to grow stronger and more resilient in the face of adversity.

The impact of bipolar disorder on a relationship can manifest in several ways. Mood swings can create sudden extremes of emotional climates, sometimes warm and sunny, other times cold and stormy. This unpredictability can be confusing and exhausting for a partner who might feel they're constantly walking on eggshells. During manic episodes, increased impulsivity or grandiosity can lead to decisions that strain the relationship, from extravagant spending sprees to emotional outbursts. Conversely, during depressive phases, the withdrawal and lack of energy can leave partners feeling sidelined, helpless, or neglected. The key here is understanding these impacts and actively working together to mitigate them.

One effective strategy for couples navigating these turbulent waters is couples therapy. It's like having a skilled guide for your relationship journey, someone who can help map out the emotional terrain of bipolar disorder and equip both partners with the tools they need to navigate it. Therapy provides a neutral ground to explore sensitive issues, improve communication skills, and strengthen emotional connections. It's about expressing needs and frustrations without blame and listening empathetically. Couple therapy can also be a space to develop strategies tailored to your relationship, helping you foresee and manage potential conflicts arising from bipolar symptoms.

Establishing routines can also play a crucial role in stabilizing relationship dynamics. Just as personal routines aid in managing bipolar disorder, relationship routines can help maintain a sense of normalcy and security. This could be as simple as setting aside time daily to connect without distractions, engaging in a shared hobby, or maintaining a date night each week. These routines become shared anchors, points of stability, and predictability amidst the unpredictability of bipolar disorder. They offer moments of connection that can reinforce the partnership, providing reassurance and continuity that can be crucial during challenging times.

Maintaining intimacy is another crucial aspect, often directly impacted by the symptoms of bipolar disorder. The fluctuations in emotional and physical intimacy can be one of the most challenging aspects for couples. During manic or depressive episodes, sexual desire can either spike or plummet, creating mismatches in libido that can frustrate both partners. Open discussions about sexual needs and expectations can help, as can scheduling intimacy in some cases, which might not sound romantic but can be surprisingly effective in ensuring both partners' needs are met. It's also essential to foster emotional intimacy, ensuring that physical closeness is just one aspect of a deeper emotional connection. Small gestures of affection, active listening, and verbal affirmations of love and commitment can all nurture this emotional closeness, maintaining a bond that physical intimacy alone cannot sustain.

Lastly, the role of external support systems cannot be overstated. No couple is an island; sometimes, the best support comes from outside the relationship. Encouraging each other to maintain individual friendships and hobbies can provide external outlets and perspectives that enhance personal well-being and, by extension, relationship health. Support groups for couples dealing with bipolar disorder can also be invaluable, offering a community that understands and shares similar challenges. These groups can provide practical advice and emotional support, reduce feelings of isolation, and provide examples of successful coping strategies.

In essence, managing bipolar disorder within a relationship is about teamwork, where both partners actively engage in strategies that foster understanding, stability, and growth. It's about turning challenges into opportunities to strengthen the bond, ensuring the relationship survives and thrives. By embracing therapies, establishing routines, maintaining open communication about intimacy, and leveraging external supports, couples can navigate the complexities of bipolar disorder together, preserving the harmony and deepening the connection that initially brought them together.

6.3 Parenting with Bipolar: Guidance and Support Strategies

Parenting is akin to being a superhero; it's a role filled with challenges, rewards, and the occasional need to save the day. When you add bipolar disorder into the mix, the cape feels a bit heavier, and the days can sometimes seem a bit more daunting. But fear not because, with the right strategies, you can navigate the complexities of parenting with bipolar disorder, ensuring that you manage your health while providing a loving, stable environment for your kids.

Let's talk about balancing parenting and bipolar management. Imagine you're juggling—each ball represents different aspects of your life: one for parenting, one for work, another for personal relationships, and a brightly colored one for managing bipolar disorder. Keeping all these in the air can be tricky, especially when the bipolar ball feels like it's made of lead some days. The key here is not to prioritize one ball over the others but to learn techniques that help you juggle them more effectively. This starts with a solid routine that includes time for medication, therapy sessions, and rest. It's also crucial to stay vigilant about your symptoms; being proactive about managing your health can prevent your symptoms from overshadowing your parenting. Maintain open lines of communication with your mental health provider about how parenting impacts your bipolar disorder and vice versa. This ongoing dialogue can help tailor your treatment plan to fit your lifestyle as a parent better.

Communicating with children about bipolar disorder can feel as tricky as explaining why the sky is blue; it's complex but not impossible. The goal is to provide them with honesty, reassurance, and support. Start by considering your child's age and maturity level. Younger kids need more straightforward explanations—perhaps explaining that sometimes you have "big feelings" or "energy days" and other times you might feel "slow" or "sad." It's like explaining weather patterns: sunny days, stormy days, and everything. For older children and teenagers, you can share more detailed information, perhaps comparing bipolar disorder to a medical condition that requires ongoing treatment, much like diabetes or hypertension. Regardless of age, reassure them that your mood changes are not their fault, nor are they responsible for managing them. This reassurance can be a massive relief for kids who may not fully understand the complexities of mental health.

Creating a supportive family environment is crucial. This doesn't mean turning your home into a fortress but setting up structures that foster stability. Routines are potent for children; they provide security and normalcy. Keep regular meal times, bedtimes, and family activities, even if your mood fluctuates. These predictable patterns can be comforting, not just for your children but for you as well. Also, consider having a plan in place for times when your bipolar disorder might disrupt this routine. This could involve arranging for a family member or a trusted friend to step in when you need to focus on your health. Additionally, have emergency plans that your children understand, such as who to call if they need help when you cannot provide it due to your symptoms.

Seeking and accepting help might be among the toughest yet most critical strategies. It's not uncommon to feel like you have to do it all, especially as a parent. But remember, asking for help isn't a sign of weakness—it's an act of strength. When things feel overwhelming, lean on your partner, relatives, or close friends to share the load. Professional services like therapists or parenting counselors can provide guidance and support tailored to your needs. Moreover, consider joining support groups for parents with bipolar disorder. Sharing your experiences and hearing others' can give practical advice and emotional solace that you're not alone in this journey.

In navigating the dual challenges of parenting and managing bipolar disorder, remember that perfection is not the goal; presence is. It's about being there, doing your best, and showing up for your kids, even on days when you don't feel like you can. By managing your health, communicating openly, creating a supportive environment, and seeking help when needed, you're not just surviving as a parent with bipolar disorder; you're thriving, providing your children with the resilience and understanding they need to navigate their own lives.

6.4 Supporting a Partner or Family Member with Bipolar

Stepping into the shoes of someone who supports a loved one with bipolar disorder is a bit like becoming an impromptu juggler at a circus. One moment, you're a spectator, and the next, you're keeping several balls in the air—emotional support, daily responsibilities, and sometimes crisis management—all while trying to maintain your own balance. Understanding bipolar disorder from the outside involves recognizing that this isn't just a series of mood swings but a complex and enduring condition that your loved one battles with. It requires a deep dive into the symptoms, which fluctuate from the highs of mania to the lows of depression, each bringing its own set of challenges.

For starters, education is vital. The more you know about bipolar disorder, the better equipped you are to provide support that's both effective and empathetic. Recognize the symptoms that come with each phase. Manic episodes might include increased energy, less need for sleep, and sometimes reckless behavior, while depressive episodes can bring overwhelming sadness, fatigue, and withdrawal. Understanding these signs helps you to not misinterpret these behaviors as personal or intentional but as part of a medical condition.

Now, let's talk about the fine line between supporting and enabling. It's like knowing when to offer a helping hand and when to encourage them to walk on their own. For instance, during a manic phase, it might be instinctive to want to protect your loved one from impulsive decisions. However, it's crucial to encourage strategies they can employ, like discussing a spending limit or identifying activities that channel their energy in healthier ways. In contrast, during depressive episodes, support might look like ensuring they're not isolating themselves excessively while respecting their need for space and quiet. It's about empowerment, not control—helping them manage their symptoms without taking over their responsibilities, which can undermine their confidence and ability to cope independently.

Caring for the caregiver—you—is not just a sidebar in this narrative; it's central to the plot. Supporting someone with bipolar disorder can be draining, both emotionally and physically. You must carve out time for self-care, ensuring you don't burn out. Set boundaries that help you maintain a healthy balance. This might mean setting times when you focus on your own needs or hobbies, or it might involve seeking support from others, such as friends, family, or support groups. As an emergency oxygen mask on a plane, you must secure your mask before assisting others. This ensures you have the strength and emotional capacity to support your loved one's needs.

Preparing for emergencies is another critical aspect. Bipolar disorder can sometimes lead to crises, such as severe depressive episodes or even suicidal ideation. Having a plan in place can be a lifesaver. This includes knowing when and how to contact healthcare providers, understanding what to say and do in a crisis, and having a list of emergency contacts, including close friends, family, or a therapist. It's like having a map and a first aid kit ready; you hope never to need them, but should the situation arise, you're prepared. This preparation provides a practical framework for handling such situations and gives you peace of mind, knowing you're not navigating this terrain without tools.

Supporting a loved one with bipolar disorder is a profound journey of love, patience, and understanding. It requires you to be informed, empathetic, and resilient. You ensure your support is sustainable and effective by educating yourself, balancing supporting and enabling, caring for your emotional needs, and preparing for potential crises. Remember, your role is pivotal—helping your loved one manage their disorder and walking alongside them with strength, compassion, and hope, making the journey less daunting for you both.

6.5 The Social Life Spectrum: Maintaining Friendships

Managing friendships when you're juggling the highs and lows of bipolar disorder can sometimes feel like trying to sing a duet solo— tricky, if not downright disheartening. The challenges are real, from the urge to hibernate during a depressive spell to the whirlwind of over-sharing during a manic phase. It's like your social skills are on a seesaw, and finding that balance is imperative to maintaining meaningful relationships that don't just survive but thrive, even in the face of bipolar disorder.

Let's unpack this, starting with the challenges. When you're low, the world seems to be moving slowly, and isolation is the only comforting response. It's not that you don't value your friends; it's just that the energy required to engage can feel as draining as running a marathon. On the flip side, during manic episodes, you might find yourself the life of the party, but the intensity can be overwhelming for others, and impulsivity can lead to actions that strain friendships. These fluctuations can make friendships feel like a roller-coaster ride for which not everyone is strapped in.

Building and nurturing friendships requires a toolkit, not just good intentions. Transparency is your first tool. It involves being honest about your bipolar disorder with close friends. This doesn't mean your condition needs to be the center of every conversation. However, letting friends know what you're dealing with can demystify your behaviors and help them understand your needs and boundaries. For instance, explaining that sometimes you need to step back for self-care during depressive episodes can help them understand your absences aren't about them. It's about caring for your mental health.

Communication, your next tool, is about keeping the lines open. Regular check-ins with friends, even if it's just a text or a shared meme, can keep the connection alive even when you're not up for social outings. It's also about expressing appreciation for their patience and understanding, which can reinforce their support and willingness to stand by you. Mutual support is crucial; it's a two-way street. Just as you appreciate their understanding, offering an empathetic ear or support during their times of need can strengthen the bond, making the friendship a shared refuge and joy, not just a support group.

Now, let's talk about social activities. Choosing suitable activities can play a significant role in managing your symptoms while still engaging with friends. Opt for low-pressure environments that allow you to engage at your own pace. Group activities like art classes, book clubs, or nature walks can be great because they offer both social interaction and the opportunity to withdraw into the activity when you feel overwhelmed. These settings can be less emotionally demanding but provide the social stimulation crucial for mental health.

Dealing with rejection or loss of friendships is perhaps the most challenging part. Not everyone will understand or stick around, and that's a tough pill to swallow. It's important to grieve these losses, to allow yourself to feel the sadness or frustration, and to recognize that it's not a reflection of your worth. Friendships can end for many reasons, and bipolar disorder might be one factor. The key is to cherish the friends who stick around, those who accept you with all your facets, and remain open to new relationships. Remember, the quality of friendships often matters much more than quantity. Each true friend is a treasure, a vital piece of your support network that helps you navigate the complexities of life with bipolar disorder.

Operating in the social spectrum with bipolar disorder isn't about perfection; it's about effort, understanding, and a bit of strategy. By being honest, maintaining communication, choosing the correct social settings, and handling losses gracefully, you can cultivate a circle of friends that enriches your life and anchors you through the storms. Friendships, like gardens, require tending, and with the proper care, even a garden touched by the wild swings of bipolar disorder can flourish, bringing color and joy to your life.

6.6 Bipolar and Isolation: Breaking the Cycle

Let's face it, sometimes dealing with bipolar disorder feels a bit like you're a smartphone in airplane mode: disconnected from the world and not entirely functioning at total capacity. Isolation isn't just about being alone; it's a whole mood, and for someone with bipolar disorder, it can be a frequent guest. The reasons? They're as complex as a well-aged bourbon. Stigma, for starters, plays a significant role. That pesky voice whispers, "They won't understand," or "They'll think you're crazy," pushing you to pull back from social interactions. Then there's the internal duo of fear and judgment, always ready to party, making you doubt every social impulse you have. And let's not forget the symptoms themselves—when you're riding the highs of mania or sinking into the lows of depression, reaching out can feel as daunting as skydiving without a parachute.

But here's the kicker: isolation, while it might feel comforting at the moment, can feed into the very symptoms you're trying to manage. It's a classic catch-22. The good news? You can break this cycle. It starts with understanding the triggers for your withdrawal. Is it anxiety about being judged? Exhaustion from doing emotional gymnastics? Identifying these triggers is like being handed a map in a dense forest; it doesn't clear the trees but shows you a path out.

Now, let's move on to strategies to dodge the isolation bullet. First up, support groups. These aren't just about sitting in a circle and sharing your deepest fears (though that can be part of it). They're about finding your tribe, people who nod and say, "Me too" instead of "Really?" These groups provide a platform to connect, share experiences, and offer mutual support, whether face-to-face or online. It's like having a safety net for people who get it.

Community activities can also be a game-changer. Think about what you love doing or something you've always wanted to try. Photography? Hiking? Cooking? Community classes or groups focused on these interests can be a double win. You get to do something you enjoy (or think you might want) and meet people with similar interests. It's socializing with a side of distraction, which can make it feel less intense and more manageable.

Online socialization is another tool in your kit. In the digital age, connecting with others can be as easy as tapping on a screen. Online forums, social media groups, or even gaming communities can offer connections that don't require you to leave your comfort zone physically. It's like dipping your toes in the social pool without diving headfirst. Just be mindful of the nature of these interactions and aim for healthy, supportive connections.

Lastly, let's talk about reaching out. Sometimes, the most challenging part of dealing with isolation is taking that first step to connect or reconnect with others. Whether it's a text to a friend you haven't spoken to in a while, joining a new online forum, or even seeking out a mental health professional, each action can be a step away from isolation. Remember, reaching out is not a sign of weakness; it's an act of strength. It's acknowledging that everyone needs a helping hand sometimes. And in most cases, people are more understanding and supportive than you might fear.

Crafting a personalized plan to combat isolation can serve as your road map. Start by listing your triggers and the signs that you're withdrawing. Then, detail steps you can take when you notice these signs, like reaching out to a friend, attending a support group, or engaging in a community activity. Also, list the people and resources you can turn to for support. Having this plan written down can make it feel more concrete and more doable. It's like having a recipe; you might not follow it to the letter every time, but it gives you a foundation to start from, and sometimes, that's all you need to get the ball rolling.

In wrapping up this discussion on isolation and bipolar disorder, remember this: isolation can be a part of living with bipolar disorder, but it doesn't have to define your experience. I know I wrote about communication in an earlier chapter, but I cannot stress enough the importance of open communication. By understanding its roots, employing strategies to maintain connections, reaching out when needed, and having a plan, you can keep the doors open to the world around you, ensuring that isolation is a visitor, not a permanent resident. As we close this chapter and look ahead, let's carry forward the theme of connection—not just as a strategy but as a way of life, enriching our journey and enhancing our resilience in managing bipolar disorder. Let's stay connected, stay engaged, and continue supporting each other in every way possible.

Addressing Stigma and Building Advocacy

Imagine you're at a party, and instead of saying, "Hi, I'm Jane, I like hiking, and I'm allergic to peanuts," you say, "Hi, I'm Jane, and I have bipolar disorder." You can almost hear the record scratch, right? That's stigma for you—turning what could be a conversation into a conversation stopper. Stigma is like that unwelcome party guest who whispers tall tales about you in every corner of the room. It's pervasive, sticky, and, frankly, a real pain to deal with. But here's where we start changing the tune, turning down the volume on stigma and cranking up the dialogue on advocacy. In this chapter, we will unpack the suitcase of stigma, lay everything out, and see how we can fold it up neatly into something manageable, maybe even something positive.

7.1 Fighting the Stigma: Strategies for Personal Advocacy

Understanding Stigma

Stigma doesn't materialize out of thin air. It's woven from threads of misunderstanding, fear, and stereotypes, all dyed in the deep hues of historical prejudice. It's like a bad game of telephone; somewhere along the line, the message about what bipolar disorder is got garbled up with myths, leading to a lot of confused and harmful perceptions. These perceptions can manifest in various arenas of life, causing individuals to hesitate before seeking help or, worse, to face discrimination in their social circles, workplaces, and even healthcare settings. For example, "Mental illness is due to drug or alcohol abuse."; or "Folks on disability due to mental health are living comfortably at taxpayers' expense"; "Depressed people are just weak."; "Depressed people need to try harder, pray more, snap out of it"; "Mental illness means constant hospitalization, homelessness, unemployment."

The media hasn't always been the best ally, either. How often have you seen a movie where the 'crazy' character is the villain or the comic relief, and they happen to have bipolar disorder? Quite a few, right? These portrayals stick in people's minds, coloring their perceptions of what bipolar disorder is, which leads to stigma. It'speopl a cycle that perpetuates itself, keeping those with the disorder in the shadows, often ashamed and isolated.

Personal Advocacy Techniques

So, how do you fight this Goliath? Start with the stone of knowledge. Educating yourself about bipolar disorder is like arming yourself with a shield; it protects you from internalizing the stigma and prepares you to educate others. The more you know, the more you can challenge the myths when you encounter them. Speaking of challenges, personal advocacy is all about speaking up. It's about correcting misconceptions when you hear them and sharing your own experiences if you're comfortable. Imagine turning your story into a bridge for understanding. By sharing, you humanize the condition and turn statistics into a face, a voice, and a story—stories are harder to ignore or stigmatize.

Role of Language in Combating Stigma

Never underestimate the power of words. They can build worlds or tear them down. When talking about bipolar disorder, the words you choose matter. Instead of saying someone is 'bipolar,' it's more respectful to say someone 'has bipolar disorder.' Why? Because their condition defines no one. It's about putting the person before the disorder, emphasizing that having bipolar disorder is just one aspect of their being. This might seem like a slight shift, but it's powerful because it challenges the subconscious notions that link identity closely with disorder.

Engagement in Advocacy Activities

If you're feeling fired up and ready to take your advocacy to the next level, why not dip your toes into broader advocacy activities? This could be anything from participating in mental health awareness campaigns, volunteering for organizations that support those with bipolar disorder, or even starting a blog or podcast. Every action, no matter how small, ripples outwards. It's about creating waves in the stagnant waters of stigma, showing that those with bipolar disorder aren't just surviving; they're thriving, leading, and changing the narrative.

We can shift perceptions by understanding stigma, harnessing the power of educated advocacy, carefully choosing words, and actively engaging in advocacy efforts. It's about painting a new picture, one where bipolar disorder is seen not just with understanding and empathy but as an integral part of the diverse human tapestry. Let's keep the conversation going, challenge the myths, and keep pushing for a world where no one has to whisper their diagnosis at a party—or anywhere else.

7.2 Educating Others: How to Share Your Story Effectively

When you decide to share your story of living with bipolar disorder, it's like deciding to let someone read a few pages of your diary. It's intimate, it's revealing, and yes, it can be a bit scary. However, the power of personal stories in breaking down barriers and fostering understanding cannot be overstated. Each time someone bravely shares their experience, the cloak of mystery that surrounds bipolar disorder gets a little lighter. It's about putting a human face on a condition often shrouded in myths and misconceptions, transforming abstract statistics into something palpable, honest, and relatable. Washington State has a group called "Stand up for Mental Health." It is a comedy group founded by David Granirer. From their website, "it's a comedy therapy program teaching stand-up comedy to people with mental illness or mental health issues as a way of building confidence and fighting public stigma." You can read more at http://standupformentalhealth.com/

There are many ways to tell your story while helping yourself and others. Another source of reliable information is the National Alliance on Mental Illness (NAMI). You can read more about them at their website: https://www.nami.org/

Now, let's navigate the hows. Sharing your story is not just about what you say but how you say it, where you say it, and who you say it to. The platform you choose can make a big difference. Are you more comfortable writing a blog post, speaking at a community event, or perhaps sharing through a video on social media? Each medium reaches a different audience and comes with its own dynamic. For instance, writing gives you the time to choose your words carefully and to edit your thoughts for clarity and impact, while speaking directly to an audience can create an immediate, emotional connection that is both powerful and persuasive.

Setting boundaries is crucial for your emotional well-being. Before you share, decide how much you're comfortable revealing. It's okay not to divulge every detail; share what feels right for you. Consider preparing answers to potential questions from your audience, which can help steer the conversation toward areas you're comfortable discussing. And remember, you have the right to say, "I'd prefer not to go into detail about that." This protects you from feeling exposed or vulnerable beyond what you're prepared for.

Facing backlash is a reality for many who share their stories, especially on social media platforms where anonymity can embolden negativity. Prepare yourself for this possibility by bracing for it and cultivating a support network—friends, family, or a therapist—who can offer you a boost if things get tough. Focus on the positive impact your story may have. For every negative comment, there's a chance someone else feels seen, understood, or inspired to seek help because of your words. Keep your focus on these potential positives; let them be the wind in your sails against the rough waves of criticism.

Encouraging others to share their stories can multiply the impact of your advocacy. When one person speaks up, others are encouraged to do the same. If you can, foster an environment where sharing is supported and valued. This could be in a support group setting, through a blog or podcast, or at community events. Highlight the benefits of sharing—not just in educating others and reducing stigma but in personal empowerment and community building. Your story is a powerful beacon; it can light the way for others, showing them that they're not alone in their struggles and that their voices, too, have power.

In sharing your story, you're doing more than recounting events; you're changing the narrative around bipolar disorder, challenging stigma, and paving the way for a more understanding and supportive society. It's about turning your experiences into tools of education and instruments of change, and in doing so, you not only help others but also empower yourself. Through this act of bravery, you reclaim your narrative and remind us of the incredible resilience and diversity of the human spirit. So, share wisely, protect your peace, and remember that your story can enlighten, inspire, and transform, one word at a time.

7.3 Mental Health in the Workplace: Rights and Advocacy

Tiptoeing around the topic of bipolar disorder at work might feel like trying to dance ballet on a tightrope—high stakes, high stress, and a genuine fear of falling. But let's lace up those shoes and find a safer way to navigate workplace disclosure because, really, you deserve to work in an environment where you don't have to hide a part of who you are. Let's break down the intricacies of revealing your bipolar disorder at the office. Imagine this: You're armed with a toolkit, each tool representing a different aspect of the disclosure process. First up, timing—choosing when to disclose is like finding the right moment to jump into double Dutch. It's about finding that sweet spot where you feel secure in your role and trust the dynamics within your team.

Now, consider the pros and cons like you're weighing apples against oranges. On the one hand, disclosing can lead to accommodations that make your daily grind more manageable—think flexible hours or a quiet workspace away from the bustling open office. Conversely, there's always the risk of stigma, those old whispers of misunderstanding that might color colleagues' perceptions of your capabilities. It's a tough call, but knowledge is your safety net here. Understanding your company's policies on mental health can provide a solid foundation, showing you where and how the firm stands on supporting employees like you.

Rolling into the territory of legal rights feels like pulling on a superhero cape—suddenly, you're not just an employee but an employee backed by the law. In many regions, disability and employment laws, like the Americans with Disabilities Act (ADA) in the U.S., are there to protect you from discrimination. They ensure you can request reasonable accommodations without fear of retribution. But what does that look like in real life? It's not about dramatic gestures; it's the simple things like adjusting your work schedule to accommodate therapy sessions or even transitioning to a quieter part of the office to help you focus when you're navigating a depressive phase.

Advocating for mental health policies in your workplace can sometimes feel like you're trying to move a mountain. But remember, even mountains erode over time, especially when hit by the persistent flow of advocacy. Start small—maybe it's initiating a conversation with HR about mental health resources or organizing a workshop on mental health awareness. Every small action adds a layer to the foundation of a more understanding and supportive work environment. Think of it as planting seeds; with patience and care, these efforts can grow into a garden where diversity and mental wellness thrive.

Building this supportive environment doesn't require grand gestures. Sometimes, it's as simple as fostering open conversations about mental health or sharing resources and stories that humanize mental health challenges. It's about changing the narrative to move away from stigma and towards understanding and support. Consider this: if every workplace embraced even a fraction of these approaches, we could transform corporate cultures worldwide, making them bastions of support and understanding.

Navigating the complexities of mental health advocacy in the workplace is no small feat. Still, equipped with the proper knowledge, a clear understanding of your rights, and a strategy for advocacy, you can create waves of change, not just for yourself but for everyone who might feel like they're walking that tightrope alone. Let's keep pushing for workplaces that aren't just about productivity but also about people—where every employee has the support they need to survive and thrive.

7.4 Joining the Wider Conversation: Community and Advocacy

Imagine if every voice that ever felt stifled by the weight of bipolar disorder could join in a harmonious chorus, singing out not just for awareness but for action and change. That's the power of community involvement, a force that amplifies individual whispers into a roar that can't be ignored. When you step into the sphere of local and online bipolar disorder communities, you're not just entering a support group; you're stepping into a powerhouse of collective experience and advocacy. Here, every shared story, every exchanged tip, every word of encouragement acts like a thread, weaving a stronger safety net for all its members.

Now, think about this: each community event you participate in and each discussion you engage in adds momentum to the broader mission of destigmatizing bipolar disorder. It's like each of us holds a puzzle piece, and by coming together, we start seeing the complete picture, not just of the challenges but also of the potential for change. Local chapters of national mental health organizations often hold meetings, workshops, and public events. Getting involved in these activities allows you to connect with others navigating similar paths, perhaps in slightly different shoes. These interactions can be eye-opening, providing fresh perspectives and innovative approaches to managing bipolar disorder that you might not have considered before.

Shifting gears, let's talk about the digital age's superpower—social media. It's a tool that can broadcast your voice far beyond your local community, reaching across cities, countries, and continents. When used effectively, social media platforms become stages for advocacy and awareness, where your experiences and insights can touch lives in places you've never been. Here's the trick: maintaining a balance between being open and protecting your privacy is crucial. Deciding how much or little you want to share is perfectly okay. The goal is to foster understanding and support, not to overshare to the point where you feel exposed. You might consider using platforms that allow you to control who sees your posts or create content that focuses on general education and awareness. Keep your details vague but your message clear.

Collaborating with mental health organizations can significantly boost your advocacy efforts. These organizations often have the resources, networks, and platforms to help propel your message to a broader audience. These collaborations can be mutually beneficial if you contribute to their blogs, speak at their events, or even lead a workshop. You bring authentic, personal experience to the table, which enriches their programs and makes their outreach more relatable and impactful.

Now, let's widen the lens even further and consider the global and cultural perspectives on bipolar disorder. This disorder does not recognize borders or cultural lines; it is a universal human experience that varies only in how different cultures understand and address it. By learning about and integrating these diverse perspectives into your advocacy efforts, you're broadening your understanding and enriching the global dialogue on mental health. It helps to remember that in some cultures, mental health may still be a taboo subject, where discussions might be more restrained and require a sensitive approach. Being aware of and respectful of these differences can make your advocacy more inclusive and effective.

Engaging in these broader conversations about bipolar disorder and mental health not only strengthens your support network but also contributes to a more significant movement toward acceptance and change. It's about building bridges, opening dialogues, and ensuring the conversation around bipolar disorder is inclusive, informed, and impactful. By joining this more comprehensive conversation, you help ensure that the future of mental health advocacy is vibrant, diverse, and rich with the voices of those who live with these experiences every day. Let's keep the conversation growing louder and more inclusive with each new voice joining in.

7.5 Using Social Media for Support and Awareness

Ah, social media—where else can you find cat videos, culinary masterpieces, and meaningful mental health support all in the same place? It's a landscape where hashtags can start movements, and a single post can echo through the lives of thousands. For those navigating the waves of bipolar disorder, social media offers both a beacon of support and a platform for advocacy. But, as with any powerful tool, the key lies in using it wisely and well.

The Role of Social Media

Think of social media as a global coffee shop where conversations about mental health can happen openly and honestly. It's transformed from just a place to share selfies and gourmet meals to a significant arena for mental health discourse, providing those with conditions like bipolar disorder a space to connect, learn, and feel less alone. For instance, hashtags like #BipolarDisorder or #MentalHealthAwareness can lead you to a treasure trove of stories, advice, and support from all corners of the globe. It's about turning isolation into community, giving you a sense of solidarity that can be hard to find offline.

Social media also serves as a critical platform for raising public awareness about bipolar disorder. Through campaigns, shared articles, and personal stories, it can educate a broad audience about the realities of living with bipolar disorder, chipping away at the stigma. Each shared experience helps paint a more comprehensive, more nuanced picture of what bipolar disorder really looks like, breaking down misconceptions and fostering a more informed public dialogue. It's like each post, each tweet and each story is a brushstroke in a much larger mural depicting the true face of mental health.

Creating Engaging Content

Creating content that resonates and educates isn't just about pouring your heart out on the keyboard. It's about crafting your message in a way that engages and informs. Start with authenticity— be true to your experiences and feelings. Authenticity resonates; it cuts through social media noise like a bell. Combine this with educational tidbits, like quick facts about bipolar disorder or debunking myths. Imagine you're creating a mini-infographic in each post. For example, a simple, eye-catching image paired with a caption, "Did you know bipolar disorder affects over 5 million adults in the U.S. alone? Let's talk about it!" can grab attention and spread knowledge.

But let's spice it up a bit. Humor, when appropriate, can be a powerful tool. A light-hearted meme about the ups and downs of bipolar disorder can not only bring a smile but also make a point in a relatable way. Visual content, like videos or themed photo series, can boost engagement. Maybe it's a video diary of a week in your life with bipolar disorder or a series of portraits of individuals thriving despite their diagnosis—visual stories that invite viewers into your world.

Navigating Online Communities

Finding the right online community is like finding the right coffee shop. You want a place where you feel comfortable, where the vibe is supportive, and where the baristas (or moderators, in this case) ensure a safe, welcoming environment. Start by exploring groups focused on mental health, particularly those that cater to bipolar disorder. Read the posts, check the interactions, and understand the community's tone and rules.

Once you've found a community that feels like a good fit, jump in—but remember, it's about both giving and taking. Share your experiences and support, and seek advice and camaraderie when needed. Engage respectfully, remembering that every member is navigating their challenges. This give-and-take strengthens the fabric of these communities, weaving a network of support that extends far beyond the screen.

Digital Self-Care

But here's the thing—while social media can be a lifeline, it can also be a whirlpool, pulling you into depths of negativity or oversharing. That's where digital self-care comes into play. It's about setting boundaries for how much time you spend online and being mindful of how this time affects your mood. Notice when exposure to certain content triggers negative feelings or exacerbates your symptoms. When this happens, give yourself permission to step back, unfollow, or mute accounts that impact your mental health negatively.

Take regular breaks. Like any space, social media can feel overwhelming. Schedule 'offline' periods into your day to disconnect from the digital world and reconnect with the physical one. Go for a walk, meditate, or bask in a few quiet moments—whatever helps you reset. Remember, the online world will still be there when you return, but your well-being must come first.

Navigating social media as someone with bipolar disorder means balancing its benefits with its challenges. By understanding its role, creating engaging and authentic content, actively participating in supportive communities, and practicing diligent digital self-care, you harness this modern tool for support, education, and connection, turning what could be a battleground into a haven. In this place, understanding and community flourish.

7.6 The Power of Peer Support: Finding and Offering Help

Imagine walking into a room where everyone speaks your language, not just linguistically but emotionally and experientially. That's what a good peer support group feels like for someone with bipolar disorder. It's a place where the walls come down, you can share without fear of judgment, and the nods of understanding are as comforting as a cozy blanket on a chilly evening. Peer support groups provide a unique blend of empathy, shared experiences, and collective wisdom that can be a lifeline in managing the complexities of bipolar disorder.

The beauty of peer support lies in its foundation of mutual understanding. Here, you're not just receiving support; you're surrounded by individuals who get the highs and lows because they've ridden similar roller-coasters. This environment fosters a deep sense of community and belonging, which can be incredibly validating when you feel isolated by your condition. The shared stories and strategies can also be enlightening, offering new perspectives and coping mechanisms that might not have crossed your radar otherwise. It's like having a living library at your fingertips, where the books breathe and speak, each one offering insights into different chapters of managing bipolar disorder.

But how do you find the right group? It's a bit like dating—you might need to meet a few before you find the one that clicks. Start by searching for local support groups in your community. Hospitals, mental health clinics, and organizations dedicated to bipolar disorder often host or direct you to existing groups. Online platforms can also be goldmines for peer support. Websites devoted to mental health and social media groups offer virtual communities that can be accessed from the comfort of your home. When selecting a group, consider the format—is it a formal meeting with a facilitator or a more casual meet-up? What's the group's policy on confidentiality, and how do they ensure a safe and supportive environment? Answering these questions can help gauge whether the group's vibe aligns with your needs and comfort level.

Transitioning from a group member to a peer supporter can be rewarding. If you find yourself drawn to the idea of guiding and supporting others through their bipolar experiences, becoming a peer supporter might be a natural next step. This role often requires some training, which many organizations provide. Training programs typically cover vital skills such as active listening, confidentiality, crisis response, and boundary-setting, preparing you to facilitate sessions effectively and empathetically. The personal benefits of this role are profound; it's not just about giving back but also about strengthening your coping strategies and resilience. Teaching is often the best way to understand a subject deeply, and by articulating and advising on coping mechanisms, you reinforce these practices in your own life.

However, as you step into a support role, remember the golden rule of peer support: boundaries. Maintaining clear boundaries ensures that your support role remains healthy and doesn't infringe on your well-being or group dynamics. It's essential to recognize the limits of your role—you're there to support, not to treat or counsel. This distinction helps prevent burnout and ensures that your involvement remains a positive force in your life and those you support.

Peer support is an invaluable facet of living with and managing bipolar disorder. It provides a platform for emotional support, personal growth, and empowerment. Whether as a member or a supporter, participating in these groups contributes to a vibrant community that thrives on shared strength and understanding. Each meeting, each story, and each shared struggle and triumph weave a more robust, supportive tapestry for everyone involved.

As we close this chapter on peer support, let's reflect on the power of shared experiences and the profound impact of empathy and understanding in managing bipolar disorder. We find both help and hope through peer support—strategies and strength. These connections remind us that we do not travel alone while our journeys are personal. Let's carry this spirit of community and support forward as we continue to explore ways to live fully and vibrantly with bipolar disorder.

Long-Term Management and Future Planning

Picture this: You've just built a spectacular sandcastle, complete with towers, a moat, and even a tiny flag on top. Now, imagine the tide is coming in. You wouldn't just leave your masterpiece to the mercy of the waves, right? You'd probably start reinforcing the walls, maybe building a barrier or two. That's a bit like managing bipolar disorder in the long run. It's about building resilience and preparing for the ebbs and flows, ensuring your hard work—your stability, your mental peace—stays intact, even when the tides of life get a little rough.

8.1 Building Resilience: Strategies for Long-Term Stability

Understanding Resilience

Let's kick off with a clear picture of what resilience means in the context of bipolar disorder. Think of resilience as your psychological immune system, a built-in buffer against the stressors and storms of life. It's not about avoiding episodes or never facing challenges—that's about as realistic as wearing bubble wrap to avoid getting bumped. Instead, resilience is about bouncing back. It's about having the tools and the toughness to get up when knocked down and learn from each experience so you're even stronger for the next round.

For anyone living with bipolar disorder, resilience is a key player. It's what turns "I can't handle this" into "I've got this." It's the difference between a setback defining your path or refining it. Building resilience means equipping yourself with strategies to navigate manic and depressive episodes and integrating practices into your life that promote long-term stability. It's about crafting a life that withstands the waves and learns to surf them.

Developing Coping Skills

Now, let's dive into the nitty-gritty of developing the coping skills that build resilience. First up is problem-solving. Life throws curve balls, and bipolar disorder might add some spin. Developing strong problem-solving skills means getting better at identifying problems (like recognizing the onset of a mood swing), brainstorming potential solutions (maybe adjusting your sleep schedule or medication), and implementing these solutions before things escalate.

Next, we have emotional regulation. It's all about managing those intense emotions without letting them tip you over. Techniques like mindfulness, deep breathing, or expressive writing can help keep your emotional boat steady in choppy waters. It's like installing a set of emotional shock absorbers ready to smooth out the jolts.

Of course, there's seeking support. Whether from friends, family, a therapist, or a support group, building a network of people who get it and have your back can make all the difference. It's like having a team in your corner, ready to pass you water and a towel and to cheer you on every step of the way.

Creating a Support System

Speaking of support, let's talk about how to build that dream team. A robust support system is more than just having people around; it's about having the right people around. Family and friends who are educated about bipolar disorder can provide not just companionship but also understanding and practical help. Healthcare providers, from your psychiatrist to your therapist, are your professional support squad, crucial for managing the clinical aspects of bipolar disorder.

But don't forget about peer support. Connecting with others walking a similar path can provide insights and empathy you might not find elsewhere. They're the ones who can say, "Me too," and mean it, who can share strategies that worked (or didn't), and who can truly understand the ups and downs you're experiencing.

Stress Management and Mindfulness

Last but not least, let's tackle stress management and mindfulness. If stress is like wind to a wildfire, then learning to manage it is crucial. Techniques like mindfulness can help you stay present and grounded, reducing overall stress and helping to mitigate triggers that might lead to mood episodes. Consider mindfulness as your mental pause button, allowing you to stop, breathe, and respond to situations more clearly rather than in haste.

Incorporating regular mindfulness practices, such as meditation, yoga, or even mindful walking, can significantly enhance your resilience. It's about creating a calm core amid life's chaos, a center from which you can operate with peace and perspective. And when the winds do pick up, you'll be ready to withstand them but to harness them, turning challenges into opportunities for growth and learning.

8.2 Anticipating and Managing Bipolar Episodes

Let's imagine for a moment that you're the captain of a ship. Navigating the ocean is like managing bipolar disorder: calm seas can turn stormy in a flash, and you might struggle to stay afloat without a good map and a solid plan. Learning to recognize the early warning signs of your bipolar episodes is akin to spotting those dark clouds on the horizon—it's your first clue that you need to prepare for rough weather. These signs can be subtle, like feeling just a bit too energetic or finding that your thoughts start racing like a sports car at a green light. Or maybe it's the opposite; things start slowing down, and getting out of bed feels as rigid as swimming through syrup.

Now, once you've spotted these signs, what's next? This is where your action plans come into play. Think of them as your navigation charts, guiding you safely through the storm. Crafting a personalized action plan involves mapping out what steps to take when symptoms begin to amplify. This might include adjusting your medication under medical guidance, scheduling extra therapy sessions, or temporarily tweaking your daily routines to reduce stress. It's about having a clear, concrete plan to act when you see those warning signs rather than waiting for the storm to hit in full force.

Engaging your support network effectively is crucial and can be delicate. Your loved ones must know what to expect and how they can assist. This isn't about them taking control but about offering support in ways that truly help. Whether giving you space when you need it, providing a listening ear, or ensuring you don't miss a medication dose, their informed, sensitive involvement can be a lifeline during turbulent times. It's about them understanding your condition well enough to offer the right kind of support at the right time, which requires open, ongoing communication. Let them know what works and what doesn't, and remember, this is a two-way street; they need your guidance as much as you need their support.

Managing medication over the long haul is another critical aspect of navigating bipolar disorder. Medications can change in effectiveness over time, and side effects can evolve. It's like maintaining your ship; it requires regular check-ups and tune-ups. Staying in close communication with your healthcare provider about how your medications affect you is essential. Sometimes, minor adjustments can significantly affect how you feel and function. It's also important to keep track of any new symptoms or changes in your health, as they can be clues that your medication needs reevaluation. Remember, this is a marathon, not a sprint, and maintaining stability often means being proactive about your treatment plan, always with the guidance of your healthcare professionals.

By recognizing early signs, having robust action plans, wisely involving your loved ones, and managing your medication effectively, you're not just reacting to the storm—you're skillfully navigating through it, keeping your ship steady and your journey on course.

8.3 The Role of Routine Medical Care in Bipolar Management

Imagine treating your bipolar disorder management like you would a high-stakes game of chess. Each piece, from your daily routines to your coping strategies, plays a crucial role. But let's not forget the king on this chessboard: routine medical care. Regular check-ups with your mental health professionals are akin to making strategic moves that keep you safe and checkmate the disorder before it can declare a victory. These appointments allow you to review your treatment progress, make necessary tweaks, and ensure everything is on track. Just like a chess master reviews past games, these sessions help you and your healthcare provider analyze what's working and what isn't, ensuring that your treatment strategy evolves as you do.

Building a collaborative relationship with your healthcare providers is like forming a dynamic duo. It's about more than just showing up; it's about engaging actively in your treatment plan. Good communication is the cornerstone here. It means being open about your feelings, asking questions, and expressing concerns about your treatment. Think of it as having a co-pilot; while in the driver's seat, your healthcare provider is there to help navigate, offering expert advice and ensuring you don't miss any turns. It can be helpful to come prepared with notes or a list of topics you want to discuss, making the most of your time during each visit. And remember, setting mutual goals during these appointments can give you clear markers of progress and success, which can be incredibly motivating as you manage your bipolar disorder.

Now, let's talk about the physical aspect of things. Monitoring and managing physical health issues that arise as side effects of bipolar disorder or its treatments are as crucial as mental management itself. Some medications might have side effects that affect your physical health, such as weight gain, sleep disturbances, or more complex metabolic changes. Regular physical check-ups, therefore, are as non-negotiable as your psychiatric evaluations. These help catch potential issues early, allowing for adjustments before they become problematic. It's like watching all parts of the engine, not just the one making the most noise.

Maintaining your mental health over the long term is an ongoing process, a continuous commitment to self-care practices, therapy, and peer support. It's about finding a rhythm in therapy sessions, perhaps discovering new coping mechanisms or exploring deeper issues that influence your condition. Peer support groups can also provide a sense of community and belonging, offering practical advice and emotional solace. Self-care practices, whether regular exercise, mindfulness meditation, or journaling, act as daily maintenance for your mental well-being, like oiling the gears of a well-used machine to keep it running smoothly.

In this ongoing game of chess, where bipolar disorder brings unexpected moves, routine medical care, collaborative relationships with healthcare providers, vigilant physical health monitoring, and steadfast mental health maintenance are your best strategies for a checkmate. By staying committed to these aspects, you ensure that your management plan is as dynamic and resilient as you are, ready to adapt and respond to whatever comes your way.

8.4 Estate and Financial Planning: Preparing for the Future

Let's talk money and future planning—two things that might not be as exciting as planning your next vacation, but trust me, they're just as important. Managing finances and planning your estate when you have bipolar disorder is a bit like being a circus ringmaster. You've got to watch all the acts, from the high-flying trapeze of investments to the juggling act of savings and the tightrope walk of budgeting. It's thrilling in its own way, especially when you get everything to work in harmony. So, let's pull back the curtain on managing this financial circus with flair and foresight.

First, achieving and maintaining financial stability is your main act. It starts with the cornerstone of any sound financial plan: budgeting. Crafting a budget isn't about restricting yourself; it's about understanding your financial flow, much like a choreographer plans out dance moves. You need to know where every dollar is going, especially since mood swings can sometimes lead to impulsive spending. Start with tracking your income and expenses. Use apps or good old spreadsheets—whatever floats your boat. See where you can cut back without cutting out joy. Remember, a good budget flexes with you, giving you room to breathe and adapt.

Now, onto saving and investing, which can be your safety net. Consider saving as packing a parachute; you hope not to need it, but it's there to save the day if you do. Start small if you have to. A little can go a long way, especially with compound interest. As for investing, it's like planting a garden. It takes patience and a bit of risk tolerance, but the payoff can be well worth it. Consider talking to a financial advisor who understands the nuances of investing while managing a condition like bipolar disorder. They can help tailor an investment strategy that matches your risk tolerance and long-term goals.

Transitioning to estate planning, this is where you get to direct how the show goes on, even if you're not around to see it. It's about making sure your assets are distributed according to your wishes and that decisions about your health and finances can be made by someone you trust if you cannot do so. Start with the basics: a will, like your script, telling everyone what you want to happen. Then, consider setting up a power of attorney and a healthcare directive. These are your backstage crew, ready to step in and ensure your wishes are respected when you can't call the shots.

Navigating insurance and planning for future care needs might not be glamorous, but it's critical. Consider insurance as your contingency plan; the understudy is ready to step in when needed. Whether it's health insurance to cover therapy sessions and medication or long-term disability insurance just in case, being covered provides peace of mind. As for future care planning, it's about looking ahead. If your condition might require long-term treatment or care, planning now can make a world of difference later. Look into long-term care options and ensure your insurance can cover the kind of care you envision for yourself.

Lastly, let's spotlight some resources and professional assistance. Managing finances and planning for the future isn't a solo act. Some professionals specialize in helping individuals with chronic conditions manage their money and plan their estates. Organizations like the National Disability Institute offer financial planning resources sensitive to the needs of those with chronic conditions. Financial advisors specializing in estate planning can also provide invaluable guidance, ensuring your financial plans are as robust as possible.

Navigating your financial future when you have bipolar disorder doesn't have to be a high-wire act performed without a net. With careful planning, a good support team, and the right tools and knowledge, you can create a financial plan that meets your needs and gives you the confidence to enjoy the present, knowing the future is well-handled. So, please take a deep breath, and let's get this show on the road. Your future self will thank you for it.

8.5 Career Planning and Bipolar: Navigating Success and Challenges

Handling a career while managing bipolar disorder is akin to sailing a ship through unpredictable seas—you need a well-calibrated compass, a precise map, and the flexibility to adjust your sails as conditions change. Setting realistic and fulfilling career goals is your compass here. It's about aligning your professional aspirations with the realities of your condition, ensuring that your career path brings satisfaction and accommodates your health needs. Think about what success means to you. Is it climbing the corporate ladder or achieving a balanced life where work is just one part of your happiness equation? Understanding your true north will guide every decision, from job choices to daily tasks.

When it comes to workplace disclosure, imagine standing at a crossroads where one path is open about your bipolar disorder, and the other is more private. Each has pros and cons; the correct path depends on your unique situation and work environment. Disclosing can open the door to support and accommodations, such as flexible working hours or a quiet workspace. However, it also involves a certain level of vulnerability, as biases and misunderstandings about bipolar disorder still exist in many workplaces. Gauge your organization's culture—are mental health matters handled with sensitivity and discretion? Your answer might determine whether you share your diagnosis or choose to keep it private. If you decide to disclose, timing is crucial; it's often best after establishing your capabilities and building a rapport with your team.

Achieving professional success involves leveraging your strengths—those unique superpowers that bipolar disorder can't touch. Maybe it's your creativity, your ability to think outside the box or your resilience. Play to these strengths. Look for roles that not only require these skills but also celebrate them. Managing stress is also part of this equation. It's like knowing when to take your foot off the accelerator at work to prevent burnout. Develop strategies such as prioritizing tasks, setting clear boundaries between work and home life, and using relaxation techniques to manage stress effectively. Additionally, utilizing workplace accommodations can be a game-changer. Whether it's a flexible schedule that aligns with your energy patterns or the ability to work from home during depressive phases, these accommodations can help you maintain stability and optimize your performance.

Now, what about those considering a career change? This can feel like rewiring your entire professional existence, but sometimes, aligning more closely with your strengths and health needs is necessary. Start by evaluating what's missing in your current role. Is it creativity, flexibility, or perhaps a supportive environment? Then, look at career paths that not only interest you but also offer the accommodations you need to manage your bipolar disorder effectively. Research is fundamental—talk to people in those fields, look up job satisfaction rates, and consider the day-to-day responsibilities. It's about finding a fit that feels as right in practice as it does on paper. As you consider this change, think about the long-term management of your disorder. Will this new path provide enough stability and support? How will it impact your routine and treatment regimen? These considerations are crucial to ensure that your career change is not just a leap in the dark but a well-informed step into a more fulfilling professional life.

Directing your career while managing bipolar disorder requires a blend of self-awareness, strategic planning, and proactive adaptation. By setting clear, realistic goals, carefully considering disclosure, leveraging your strengths, managing stress, and thoughtfully considering career changes, you create a professional life that meets your aspirations and supports your well-being. This approach allows you to survive in your career and thrive, turning challenges into opportunities and your condition into a portal for unique professional contributions.

8.6 New and Emerging Treatments: Staying Informed

Staying on top of the latest trends can sometimes feel like trying to sip from a fire hose—overwhelming. But when it comes to managing bipolar disorder, keeping up with new research and treatments isn't just valuable; it's crucial. Think of it as staying ahead in a game where the rules keep evolving. The landscape of bipolar disorder treatment is continually advancing, with fresh studies, innovative therapies, and groundbreaking technologies emerging at a pace that can be hard to keep up with, yet incredibly exciting.

First, understanding the importance of staying informed about new research and treatments for bipolar disorder is akin to knowing the weather forecast before planning a picnic. It prepares you for what's coming, helps you make informed decisions, and ensures you utilize the best tools to manage your condition effectively. New research can offer insights into better management strategies, more effective medications, or even lifestyle changes that could significantly impact your quality of life. It's about giving yourself every possible advantage in managing your health.

Let's talk about evaluating these new treatments. Not all that glitters is gold. When you come across a new treatment or therapy option, it's essential to vet its credibility and potential impact thoroughly. Start by checking if the findings are from a reputable source, such as a well-respected medical journal or a leading bipolar disorder research organization. Look into who conducted the study—consider their credentials and any potential biases they might have. Also, the size and scope of the study should be evaluated; more extensive, more diverse study populations often provide more reliable insights. Discuss these treatments with your healthcare provider to understand how they might fit into your existing management plan. Considering your specific circumstances, they can help you weigh the benefits against the risks.

Participating in clinical trials is another avenue that can be both intriguing and intimidating. Clinical trials for new bipolar treatments provide a firsthand look at up-and-coming therapies and medications. However, they're a mixed bag of potential and precaution. Additionally, participating in a clinical trial can give you access to new treatments before they are widely available. It's a chance to be on the cutting edge of science, contributing to research that might change lives, possibly even your own. On the flip side, there are risks. New treatments can have unforeseen side effects or be less effective than hoped. If you're considering a clinical trial, start by thoroughly researching the trial's scope, the treatments involved, and the institution conducting the trial. Ensure the trial is registered with a recognized medical authority and understand all the consent forms before signing on the dotted line.

Lastly, let's dive into the exciting world of technology and therapy advances. Digital tools like mood-tracking apps and teletherapy are revolutionizing how bipolar disorder is managed. Mood-tracking apps, for instance, help you monitor your emotional landscape, giving you and your healthcare provider valuable data to understand better and manage your condition. Conversely, teletherapy breaks down geographical and logistical barriers, providing access to mental health support from the comfort of your home. These technological advancements are about convenience and making comprehensive, continuous care more accessible and practical.

As we wrap up this exploration of new and emerging treatments, remember that being well-informed is your best defense in the dynamic battlefield of bipolar disorder management. It empowers you to make educated decisions about your health care, keeps you connected to the latest advancements, and ultimately supports your journey toward stability and wellness. As we look forward to the next chapter, let's carry this mindset of informed curiosity and proactive engagement, continuing to explore ways to enhance our lives despite the challenges posed by bipolar disorder.

Personal Growth and Transformation

Imagine if someone told you that the very traits attributed to your bipolar disorder could be your greatest assets. It sounds like being told your worst Monday could somehow turn into your best Saturday, right? But here's the kicker—it's true. Living with bipolar disorder molds resilience, sharpens creativity, and sculpts a unique perspective on the world that can be as valuable as any masterpiece in a gallery.

9.1 Harnessing Your Bipolar Superpowers: Creativity and Resilience

Identifying Personal Strengths

Think of your journey with bipolar disorder as an intense training program you never signed up for. Sure, it's tough. It throws a curve ball faster than a major league pitcher but also builds some serious muscle in areas of your life that others might overlook. Let's start with identifying these strengths. You've probably developed a high level of empathy, a keen sense of self-awareness, or perhaps an ability to think outside the box—highly prized qualities in many areas of life and work.

Take a moment to reflect on the times when your unique traits positively impacted your life or the lives of others. Maybe it's your empathetic nature that has deepened your relationships or your creative thinking that has solved problems at work in ways nobody else could fathom. Recognizing and embracing these strengths isn't just about feeling good about yourself—it's about structuring your life around these powers. It's like realizing you've been sitting on a pile of gold. So dig in, discover these nuggets, and put them to work.

Creativity as an Outlet

Now, about that creativity—bipolar disorder and creativity have been linked in studies and anecdotes alike, suggesting that the same fire that fuels the emotional extremes of bipolar disorder may also ignite some extraordinary creative sparks. Historical figures like Virginia Woolf and modern icons like Carrie Fisher have all channeled their tumultuous energies into creating impactful art and literature, turning their experiences with bipolar disorder into powerful expressions of human emotion.

But here's the truly remarkable part—you don't need to be a famous artist to harness this aspect of bipolar disorder. Creativity comes in countless forms, from painting and writing to cooking, gardening, coding, or even devising new ways to organize your space. Whatever form it takes for you, creativity is not just an outlet for expression; it's a form of therapy. It's a way to externalize feelings, to play with them, and to see them in a different light. So, pick up that paintbrush, spatula, or spreadsheet—whatever tools you need to transform your experiences into something uniquely yours.

Building Resilience

Building resilience might sound like one of those easier-said-than-done tasks, and in some ways, it is. It's an ongoing process, like sculpting, chipping away at the not-so-great bits to reveal a more robust and defined figure beneath. Each challenge faced and navigated in the realm of bipolar disorder serves as a chisel, defining your resilience. Strategies here are about proactive management and reactive grace under pressure—maintaining treatment, yes, but also developing coping strategies that allow you to meet and greet your challenges head-on.

This might mean setting up a daily routine that includes relaxation and mindfulness or establishing a regular check-in with yourself to assess your mental landscape. Think of resilience not just as bouncing back but as bouncing forward—using the energy from each fall to propel you into a better, stronger position.

Celebrating Uniqueness

Finally, let's talk about celebrating your uniqueness. Living with bipolar disorder can sometimes feel like you're constantly being told how different you are, and not always in a good way. But here's a radical thought: what if those differences are your superpowers? What if the very qualities that make you 'different' are what make you extraordinary?

Embrace your unique perspective on the world—it's a view that can inspire, enlighten, and even change the minds and hearts of those around you. Celebrate your ability to feel deeply, to think widely, and to choose bravely. Own your story, insights, creativity, and resilience as badges of honor. Not only do they make you who you are, but they also equip you to contribute to the world in ways no one else can.

In this chapter, we've unpacked just a few of the superpowers often accompanying bipolar disorder—creativity, resilience, and a unique perspective. As you continue to navigate your path, remember that these traits are not just byproducts of your experiences with bipolar disorder; they are integral parts of the incredible, multifaceted person you are. Celebrate them, use them, and watch how they transform not just your life but also the lives of those around you.

9.2 Bipolar Disorder and Identity: A Journey of Self-Discovery

Imagine waking up one day to find you've been wearing a slightly incorrect name tag. It's not entirely wrong, but it certainly doesn't capture everything about who you are. That's a bit like what it feels like to be defined by a bipolar diagnosis. Sure, it's one aspect of your identity, but it's not the whole story. There's an entire landscape of your personality to explore beyond the borders of bipolar disorder, and it's rich with features shaped by more than just your mental health status.

Exploring your identity beyond bipolar disorder is like setting out on a grand expedition where the goal is not to find new lands but to understand the contours of your terrain. It involves peeling back the layers of labels that life and circumstances have stuck on you and getting to the rock-solid core of your personal values, interests, and aspirations. Start by asking yourself what makes you feel alive, independent of your mental health. Is it the quiet satisfaction of reading a good book? The thrill of hiking up a challenging trail? Or the joy of a perfectly baked pie? These passions and pursuits are integral colors in the tapestry of your identity. They provide a counterbalance to the weight of a bipolar diagnosis, reminding you and the world that your identity is a spectrum of experiences, talents, and dreams.

Now, let's talk about forging a positive self-image. It's easy to fall into a whirlpool of negative self-talk, especially when you're dealing with the highs and lows of bipolar disorder. But think of your mind as a garden. Negative thoughts are like weeds that can overrun it if left unchecked. Cultivating a positive self-image starts with pulling out these weeds and planting seeds of positive affirmations in their place. Celebrate your victories, no matter how small. Have you finished a project at work? That's a win. Manage to meet a friend for coffee during a low week? Another win. These achievements, minor as they might seem, are affirmations of your capabilities and worth. Make a habit of acknowledging them. Write them down, talk about them, or take a moment to appreciate them internally. Each acknowledgment fertilizes the soil of your self-esteem, gradually growing a garden where your worth is defined by more than the shadows of bipolar disorder.

Living with bipolar disorder inevitably sculpts your character in unique ways. It teaches you empathy as you understand what it means to face struggles that are not immediately visible. It teaches you patience with yourself and others as you navigate the unpredictability of mood swings. And importantly, it builds resilience as you learn to rise, again and again, embracing both your vulnerabilities and your strengths. These qualities are not just silver linings but integral components of personal growth. They are forged in the fire of managing bipolar disorder and emerge as tools to help you connect with others, overcome challenges, and pursue your life goals with a deepened understanding of human experience.

Lastly, narrative therapy and personal storytelling are powerful tools for exploring and affirming your identity. This approach involves framing your life experiences as stories, with you as the narrator and the protagonist. Crafting your narrative can be incredibly empowering. It allows you to tell your story on your terms, to highlight the battles you've won and the lessons you've learned. It's about taking control of the narrative thread and weaving a story that acknowledges bipolar disorder as part of your plot but not the entirety of it. By doing so, you reclaim your identity from the clutches of stigma and redefine it to reflect your true self, with all its complexities and colors. Whether through writing, art, or speaking, engaging in narrative therapy helps you externalize your experiences, making it easier to see how far you've come and where you want to go next. It's not just about recounting past events; it's about scripting a future where you are the hero of your own story, equipped with a deeper understanding of your strengths and how you can use them to navigate the chapters yet to come.

9.3 From Surviving to Thriving: Real-Life Success Stories

Let's shift gears and tap into some truly motivating tales from the real world—stories of individuals who didn't just handle their bipolar disorder; they thrived because of and despite it. These narratives aren't just feel-good moments but profound lessons in perseverance, understanding, and personal triumph. Picture this: each story is a beacon, lighting up paths you might walk down, showing that the hurdles of bipolar disorder don't have to be roadblocks; they can be stepping stones to something greater.

Take, for instance, the story of Alex, a graphic designer who once saw his intense mood swings as a barrier to success in the fast-paced, highly competitive creative industry. Alex struggled initially, finding the workplace environment and the pressure to consistently perform creatively during depressive episodes overwhelming. However, his journey took a turn when he began to channel his emotional highs and lows into his creative process, using periods of mania to fuel bold, innovative designs and times of depression to deepen his work's emotional impact. His unique approach not only brought him accolades in his field but also helped his colleagues and clients appreciate the depth and authenticity of his work. The key lesson here? Alex's success came from embracing his emotional experiences as assets rather than obstacles, transforming his workflow to align with the rhythms of his mood cycles.

Then there's Jenna, a social worker whose own experiences with bipolar disorder deeply enriched her ability to empathize with her clients. Jenna's diagnosis initially felt like a stigma that might hinder her career in mental health. Yet, it became clear that her insights into mental illness were invaluable. She could connect with her clients on a level that went beyond academic knowledge or professional training; she offered understanding rooted in lived experience. By openly discussing her challenges and victories in managing bipolar disorder, Jenna not only destigmatized her condition but also inspired her clients to be more open about their struggles. Her story underscores the importance of vulnerability and authenticity in transforming personal challenges into professional strengths, fostering an environment where mental health is openly discussed and managed without shame.

In case you are curious, after 30-plus years, I finally consider myself a success only recently. After many trials and errors, I have a medication cocktail that keeps me level and functioning. I spent a long time unmedicated while in the military. I burned many bridges and made lots of bad decisions. In the end, I was medically retired for other issues. Imagine not having the internet or the wealth of information that is now available. Everyone thought I was a ticking bomb! Without knowing the reason for my behavior. I won't sit here and narrate my whole string of failures, but trust me when I say I'm textbook. Thanks to newer drugs and therapy, I can see the patterns and prepare to preempt my illness before I can make any decisions that would have lasting consequences. I journal a lot, have been trying my hand at creating art, do Pilates, and practice mindfulness these days. It's a work in progress.

Reflecting on these stories, it's evident that thriving with bipolar disorder often involves redefining success. It's about recognizing that the journey is as unique as the individual and that success may not always fit into a conventional mold. This perspective is crucial because it celebrates diversity in paths to fulfillment and achievement, acknowledging that everyone's best looks different.

Encouragement to chase after your dreams—even when the path is unpredictable and the outcomes uncertain—is a theme that resonates deeply in these stories. Consider Mark, a teacher who dreamed of starting his own school. The fluctuating energy levels and unpredictable mood swings caused by his bipolar disorder made the immense task seem daunting. However, Mark's passion for education and desire to create an inclusive learning environment drove him to pursue his dream. He learned to delegate tasks during low-energy days and capitalize on his bursts of manic energy to fuel planning and creative problem-solving. Mark's school is now a reality, providing a supportive, adaptive learning environment that caters to students with diverse needs. His experience highlights the importance of adaptability and resilience, showing that you can turn your aspirations into achievements with the right strategies and support, regardless of the hurdles you might face.

These stories, each rich with struggle, triumph, and wisdom, serve as powerful reminders of the resilience and potential of individuals navigating life with bipolar disorder. They teach us that with understanding, support, and a willingness to adapt, thriving is not just a possibility but a probable outcome. Let these narratives inspire you to look at your challenges through a lens of opportunity, reframe obstacles as growth catalysts, and pursue your dreams with renewed vigor and hope, knowing that your unique journey can lead to unexpected and fulfilling destinations.

9.4 The Positive Impact of Bipolar on Personal Relationships

Let's chat about relationships. Not just any relationships but those that blossom in the garden you've cultivated through your experiences with bipolar disorder. It might seem like a stretch to view this condition as a cultivator of more profound, meaningful connections, but stay with me here—it truly can be.

Deepening Relationships Through Vulnerability

Picture this: you're standing at the edge of a diving board—the high one. Below, your friends are treading water, looking up, encouraging you to jump. Sharing your experiences with bipolar disorder with someone is like taking that leap. It's terrifying, but it's also an incredible display of trust. And just like diving into that pool, opening up can strengthen your bonds with those around you in ways you might not expect. When you share your story, you're not just sharing the highs and lows; you're inviting someone into your inner world, giving them a backstage pass to the workings of your mind. This vulnerability can transform relationships, turning casual connections into profound sources of mutual support and understanding.

This kind of sharing does more than deepen existing bonds; it can also filter out relationships that might not be suited to withstand the complexities of your life. Think of it as relationship triage, where the strength of each bond is tested. Those who stay, listen, and support you offer a foundation of trust and empathy on which you can build a lasting and resilient relationship.

Empathy and Understanding

Living with bipolar disorder naturally cultivates a profound sense of empathy. You know what it's like to feel misunderstood, to struggle silently, or to face challenges that aren't visible to the naked eye. This can make you incredibly attuned to the struggles of others, often seeing beyond the mask they present to the world. Imagine using this superpower in your relationships. Your experiences can be a bridge to understanding and supporting your loved ones in their battles, whether they're dealing with mental health issues, personal losses, or just the everyday stressors of life.

This enhanced empathy enriches your relationships and can alter your dynamic with others, fostering a deeper mutual understanding and respect. It's a bit like having an emotional X-ray vision; you're able to see beneath the surface, to the heart of what others are feeling, which can be incredibly comforting to those you love.

Building Supportive Networks

Now, about building those supportive networks—they're essential, like having a personal team of cheerleaders, therapists, and strategists all rolled into one. Creating this network involves reaching out to others who share your sensitivity to the human condition, perhaps those you meet in therapy groups, online communities, or even within your existing social circles who demonstrate an understanding of mental health challenges.

But here's the key: these networks need to be reciprocal. They're not just about getting support but about giving it, too. It's a two-way street where care and understanding flow freely in both directions. Think of it as a garden everyone tends to, where the fruits of labor benefit all who contribute. By nurturing this network, you ensure that support is there when you need it, just as you provide a shoulder or an ear when others need it.

Positive Role Modeling

Lastly, embracing your role as a positive relationship model can have a ripple effect. By managing your bipolar disorder openly and responsibly, you demonstrate that while the disorder is a part of your life, it doesn't define your entirety. You show that it's possible to live a full, productive, and loving life, which can be incredibly inspiring to others. Whether showing resilience in the face of challenges or advocating for mental health awareness, you're setting an example that challenges stigma and encourages a broader dialogue about mental health.

In your relationships, this modeling can teach others about resilience, the importance of mental health care, and the power of empathy. It's about showing—not just telling—that it's okay to have struggles and that they don't have to overshadow your achievements or worth. By being this role model, you not only change how others view bipolar disorder but also how they treat those who live with it, fostering a more understanding and supportive community around you.

In weaving these threads of vulnerability, empathy, supportive networks, and positive role modeling into the fabric of your relationships, you transform potential obstacles into opportunities for growth and connection. It's about turning your unique challenges into strengths that support your personal journey and enrich the lives of everyone around you. Through this process, your relationships become more profound, meaningful, and resilient—true testaments to the power of openness, understanding, and mutual support.

9.5 Setting and Achieving Personal Goals with Bipolar

Navigating life with bipolar disorder often feels like you're trying to assemble a puzzle on a windy day. When you think you've got a piece in place, a gust comes along, and you're scrambling to keep everything from flying away. But here's a little secret: setting and achieving goals with bipolar isn't about avoiding the wind—it's learning to build a better puzzle board. Let's talk about real-deal strategies for setting goals that stick, no matter the weather.

First things first, the art of goal-setting when you're dealing with bipolar disorder is like being a tailor; it's all about customization. Generic goals just won't fit right. They can be too tight, leaving no room for those days when you need a little more flexibility, or too loose, failing to provide the structure you crave during chaotic times. Start by acknowledging the unique challenges and strengths that come with your bipolar disorder. Perhaps your incredible bursts of energy during manic phases could be channeled into creative projects or brainstorming sessions. In contrast, the reflective nature of your depressive phases might lend itself well to planning or reflective activities. By aligning your goals with the natural ebb and flow of your energy levels, you create a rhythm that works with your bipolar disorder, not against it.

Now, onto the balancing act. Imagine you're a DJ mixing tracks in a club. Each track represents an area of your life—health, relationships, career, hobbies. Achieving balance isn't about giving each track an equal playtime; it's about creating a harmony that feels right for you. This might mean turning up the health track when you feel an episode coming on or dialing up professional aspirations during times of stability. It's crucial to tune into your needs and adjust your life's mix accordingly. This dynamic approach lets you stay responsive to your mental health while pursuing personal growth and professional success. It also means sometimes letting one track fade into the background momentarily to focus on another, knowing you can always bring it back into the mix when the time is right.

Celebrating progress in managing bipolar disorder is like cheering for every mile in a marathon, not just the finish line. No matter how small, every step forward is a victory worth recognizing. Did you make it through a tough week without canceling a single plan? That's a win. Have you managed to stick to your medication schedule despite a hectic week? Another win. These moments build on each other, forming a chain of successes that, over time, reflect significant progress. Whether treating yourself to a night out or simply acknowledging your progress, the celebration reinforces positive behavior and boosts your morale. It's a way to remind yourself that while the road may be long and winding, you are indeed moving forward, one step at a time.

Adjusting goals is an inevitable part of life with bipolar disorder. Think of your goals as living entities; they grow and change as you do. What worked for you last year might not fit this year, and that's okay. The key is to stay flexible, reassess your goals regularly, and adjust them based on your current circumstances and capabilities. Maybe you set a goal to jog daily, but you're finding it clashes with your energy levels some days. Adjusting this goal to be more flexible, perhaps changing it to 'engage in physical activity' so some days that's yoga, others a walk, keeps you moving without the pressure to hit the pavement running. This flexibility respects the dynamic nature of bipolar disorder and helps prevent the frustration that can come from feeling like you're not meeting your own expectations. In this way, adjusting goals isn't a sign of setback; it's a strategy for sustainable success, ensuring your aspirations evolve in tandem with your personal journey.

When setting and achieving goals with bipolar disorder, remember that it's less about the destination and more about crafting a journey that respects your rhythms, celebrates your progress, and adapts to your growth. It's about building that puzzle board solid and steady, so no matter how windy it gets, you can keep adding pieces, watching the picture of your life come together, bit by bit.

9.6 Embracing Change: The Evolving Nature of Bipolar Management

Change, much like that one relative who never RSVPs but always shows up at family gatherings, is inevitable. Especially when you're navigating life with bipolar disorder, where change is as constant as the ebb and flow of the tides, learning to embrace this change, rather than resisting it, can transform your approach to managing bipolar disorder and enhance your personal growth. Think of change as the landscape shifting on a long road trip—yes, it can be unpredictable and sometimes challenging, but it also brings new scenery and fresh perspectives that enrich the journey.

One of the first steps in becoming friends with change is to accept that your bipolar management will evolve. What works for you now might not work next year or even next month, and that's perfectly okay. It's not a sign of failure but a natural part of living with an inherently dynamic condition. Embracing this fact can remove a lot of pressure and open you up to exploring new strategies as your needs shift. This might mean adjusting your medications as your body responds differently over time or switching up your therapy sessions as you enter different phases of your life. It's all about keeping the dialogue with your healthcare providers open and honest, ensuring that your treatment plan stays as agile and adaptable as the disorder itself.

Staying flexible with your treatment plans and personal goals isn't just practical; it's necessary. Flexibility allows you to respond to changes in your mental health landscape with grace rather than frustration. It's like being a skilled surfer, adjusting your balance and stance as the waves change. This agility in managing your disorder can be incredibly empowering. It helps you to maintain control over your well-being, even when bipolar disorder throws a curveball your way. Similarly, your personal goals might need to be fluid. Life doesn't stop when you're managing bipolar disorder; ambitions change, new opportunities arise, and challenges crop up. Keeping your goals flexible means you can recalibrate them to align with your current capabilities and life context, ensuring they remain relevant and achievable.

Incorporating new learning and experiences into your management strategy is also crucial. Just as a chef seeks out new flavors and techniques to keep their dishes exciting, staying informed about the latest research and advancements in bipolar disorder treatment can introduce new tools and options into your management arsenal. Whether it's a new type of therapy, a newly developed medication, or holistic practices that others with bipolar disorder have found helpful, integrating new knowledge not only keeps you at the forefront of managing your condition but also empowers you to make informed decisions about your health care.

Finally, adopting a growth mindset can radically change how you view the challenges posed by bipolar disorder. Instead of seeing them as roadblocks, view them as opportunities to learn and grow. This mindset encourages resilience and a positive outlook, focusing on progress and possibilities rather than limitations. Every challenge you face and navigate successfully builds your confidence and skills, proving to yourself that you can adapt and thrive, no matter what bipolar disorder throws at you. It's about celebrating each small victory and using it as a stepping stone towards more significant achievements. With a growth mindset, every experience—good or bad—is valuable to your continuous journey toward personal and mental health growth.

As this chapter wraps up, remember that embracing change, staying flexible, continuously incorporating new learning, and maintaining a growth mindset are not just strategies for managing bipolar disorder; they are approaches to life. They prepare you to not only adapt to the winds of change but to harness them, steering your ship towards new horizons filled with possibilities. As we transition into the next chapter, let's carry forward this adaptable, open, and growth-focused mindset, exploring further how these principles can be applied to navigating the broader aspects of life with bipolar disorder.

Conclusion

Well, here we are at the end of our shared roller-coaster ride—a journey through the peaks and valleys of living with bipolar disorder. From those early days of grappling with the diagnosis, feeling like you've been handed a puzzle without a picture on the box, to now, hopefully, standing a bit taller, armed with strategies, insights, and a dash of humor to tackle the days ahead.

Together, we've traversed the landscape of bipolar disorder, not just surviving but learning how to thrive. I hope I've managed to sprinkle a bit of hope and resilience throughout these pages, illustrating that with the right tools and a hefty dose of perseverance, managing bipolar disorder is not just a possibility but a palpable reality.

Knowledge truly is power—understanding the nuts and bolts of bipolar disorder, from the latest scientific research to the spectrum of effective treatment options, is crucial. It's your armor in the ongoing battle against this condition's unpredictability. And let's not forget about the superpower of self-advocacy—navigating healthcare, personal relationships, and societal stigma with confidence and clarity.

We've talked a lot about the village it takes to manage bipolar disorder effectively. Remember, no one is an island, especially when dealing with such a complex condition. Healthcare providers, family, friends, and peer support groups are your tribe. Lean on them, learn from them, and let them lift you up when it gets tough.

Lifestyle management—oh, what a difference it makes! From tweaking your diet to incorporating exercise, prioritizing sleep, and mastering the art of stress management, these are not just good habits; they're your daily doses of stability.

Now, let's talk about growth. If you ever doubted that you could flourish amidst the chaos of bipolar disorder, let's put those doubts to rest. This journey can lead to profound personal growth, creativity, and a deep empathy that transforms how you view the world and interact with others. What some see as vulnerabilities, you can wield as strengths.

As we close this chapter (literally and metaphorically), I urge you to proudly wear your advocate hat. Share your story, challenge the stigma, and be the beacon of understanding and support the world desperately needs.

But above all, carry with you a message of hope and empowerment. Yes, the road may be bumpy (and trust me, I know a thing or two about bumpy roads), but with the strategies, knowledge, and support systems we've discussed, you are more than equipped to lead a fulfilling life. Keep learning, stay adaptable, and embrace the evolution of your management strategies and personal growth.

Take a moment to reflect on how far you've come since that initial diagnosis. It's not just about managing a condition; it's about recognizing your journey and resilience and celebrating every victory, big or small.

Keep this book close as a reminder of what you've learned and as a companion for those days when you need extra support or a quick refresh on managing symptoms. Remember, managing bipolar disorder is a continuous journey, and I'm so grateful you allowed me to be a part of yours.

Thank you for your trust, your time, and your tenacity. Here's to more good days than bad, to laughter being part of the prescription, and to you—remarkable, resilient you—thriving in all your unique glory. Cheers to moving forward, one step, one laugh, one triumph at a time.

Ivette

References

- Promising new bipolar disorder study reveals structural brain changes over time https://keck.usc.edu/news/promising-new-bipolar-disorder-study-reveals-structural-brain-changes-over-time/

- Causes of Bipolar Disorder https://www.webmd.com/bipolar-disorder/bipolar-disorder-causes

- Bipolar 1 vs. Bipolar 2: Know the Difference - Healthline https://www.healthline.com/health/bipolar-disorder/bipolar-1-vs-bipolar-2

- Environmental Risk Factors for Schizophrenia and Bipolar ... https://www.ncbi.nlm.nih.gov/pmc/articles/PMC8273311/

- Diagnosing Bipolar Disorder - NYU Langone Health https://nyulangone.org/conditions/bipolar-disorder/diagnosis

- 9 Essential Coping Strategies for Bipolar Disorder https://www.healthcentral.com/slideshow/essential-coping-strategies-for-bipolar-disorder

- Balancing Bipolar Medications and Their Side Effects https://www.healthline.com/health/bipolar-disorder/managing-medication-side-effects

- How to Build a Support System For Your Mental Health https://mywellbeing.com/therapy-101/how-to-build-a-support-system

- Holistic Treatment for Mood Disorders - Alternative to Meds https://www.alternativetomeds.com/blog/holistic-treatment-for-mood-disorders/

- Lifestyle interventions for bipolar disorders: A systematic ... https://www.sciencedirect.com/science/article/abs/pii/S0149763423002269

- Evidence-Based Psychotherapies for Bipolar Disorder - FOCUS

https://focus.psychiatryonline.org/doi/10.1176/appi.focus.2
0190004

- Balancing Bipolar Medications and Their Side Effects
  https://www.healthline.com/health/bipolar-
  disorder/managing-medication-side-effects

- Accommodations for Employees with Mental Health
  Conditions https://www.dol.gov/agencies/odep/program-
  areas/mental-health/maximizing-productivity-
  accommodations-for-employees-with-psychiatric-disabilities

- 10 Tips for Facing College with Bipolar Disorder
  https://www.bphope.com/blog/10-tips-for-facing-college-
  with-bipolar-disorder/

- The Reciprocal Relationship between Bipolar Disorder and ...
  https://pubmed.ncbi.nlm.nih.gov/27862615/#:~:text=Resul
  ts%3A%20Empathy%20and%20understanding%20from,of%
  20a%20major%20mood%20episode.

- Art, creativity, and bipolar disorder
  https://www.medicalnewstoday.com/articles/bipolar-
  disorder-art

- Tips for Explaining Bipolar Disorder to Friends and Family
  https://www.healthline.com/health/bipolar-
  disorder/talking-with-loved-ones

- Supporting someone with bipolar disorder - Mind
  https://www.mind.org.uk/information-support/types-of-
  mental-health-problems/bipolar-disorder/supporting-
  someone-with-bipolar/

- Parenting with Bipolar Disorder: Coping with Risk of
  Mood ...
  https://www.ncbi.nlm.nih.gov/pmc/articles/PMC3963259/

- Bipolar Disorder and Crumbling Relationships: Coping With
  a Bipolar Loved One
  https://highconflictinstitute.com/mental-health/bipolar-
  disorder-and-crumbling-relationships-coping-with-a-bipolar-
  loved-one/

- DBSA Support Groups
  https://www.dbsalliance.org/helping-a-friend-or-family-member/dbsa-support-groups/

- Find Support Groups https://www.mhanational.org/find-support-groups

- Bipolar disorder: Finding the right therapist and more
  https://www.medicalnewstoday.com/articles/right-therapist-for-bipolar-disorder

- How to Practice Self-Care with Bipolar Disorder
  https://www.healthline.com/health/bipolar-disorder/self-care

- Strategies to Reduce Mental Illness Stigma
  https://www.ncbi.nlm.nih.gov/pmc/articles/PMC8835394/

- Living with bipolar disorder: Employment and more
  https://www.medicalnewstoday.com/articles/bipolar-and-work#:~:text=The%20ADA%20protects%20people%20with,protects%20people%20with%20bipolar%20disorder.

- Bipolar Disorder: Relapse Warning Signs | Article
  https://www.therapistaid.com/therapy-guide/bipolar-early-warning-signs

- Bipolar Help: Living with Bipolar Disorder - HelpGuide.org
  https://www.helpguide.org/articles/bipolar-disorder/living-with-bipolar-disorder.htm

- Setting & Achieving Goals - Depression and Bipolar
  Support ... https://www.dbsalliance.org/setting-achieving-goals/

- Art, creativity, and bipolar disorder
  https://www.medicalnewstoday.com/articles/bipolar-disorder-art

- How Lifelong Learning Benefits Your Mental Health
  https://www.transformationsnetwork.com/post/how-lifelong-learning-benefits-your-mental-health

- Evidence-Based Psychotherapies for Bipolar Disorder - PMC
  https://www.ncbi.nlm.nih.gov/pmc/articles/PMC6999214

www.ingramcontent.com/pod-product-compliance
Lightning Source LLC
Chambersburg PA
CBHW040833010826
48978CB00012BB/741